What Page Are We On? 1. The Barbie Murders is Laugh Out Loud funny. You don't have to be rich, gay or live in Florida to appreciate the genuine humor in the situation Oscar Rogers creates for his readers in his delightfully twisted first novel. I'm so glad this is only the first in the series, because I cannot wait to read more of the adventures of Winston Clarke and his zany dysfunctional family.

—Lisa Bonnice, program host at The Shift Network and award-winning author of books including the metaphysical comedy *The Poppet Master*

WHAT PAGE
PAGE
Are We On?

1. THE BARBIE MURDERS

OSCAR ROGERS

Grateful Media

WHAT PAGE Are We On? 1. THE BARBIE MURDERS

©2023 by Oscar Rogers

First Edition: November 2023

ISBN: 979-8-9889579-1-1

Cover colors include Magenta CMYK (0, 100, 0, 0).

No dolls were harmed during the writing of this book.

For Mom and Dad

Contents

Prologue

Stephan Denino stood in the elevator donning sunglasses that squealed like a Brett Somers/Charles Nelson Reilly glamfest on *Match Game '75* ... breathing heavily, trying not to cry. "You drive. I'm a wreck. Maybe we shouldn't go."

"You can't not go to Marc's party," Edward replied.

"I don't want this to be all about me today, so not a word until the party is over," Stephan insisted.

First floor. Lobby. The elevator spoke as it stopped, and the doors opened.

The two quietly walked through the hotel and out to the valet pick up where Stephan's nautical blue Rolls-Royce Dawn was waiting. Stephan opened his murse and pulled out a $50 to hand the attendant, who recognized him. Dressed in black uniform shorts and a white polo with a Hilton Beach Resort logo stitched on the left breast, the valet hustled over to open the passenger door. Stephan thanked him, slipped him the bill, and slid comfortably onto the white leather seat. Another matching valet dashed over to the driver's door and opened it for Edward to enter.

"Let's put the top down," Stephan instructed. "I could use the fresh air."

His assistant pressed a button, and the luxury coupe became a luxurious convertible. They drove away – that is, until Edward spotted a white square tip of something tucked beneath the wiper blade.

"What is *that*?" Edward declared as he pulled to the side of Breakers Avenue and parked. He stepped out of the car, retrieved a Polaroid from the windshield, looked at it, then paused for a spell deciding if he should or shouldn't get back into the car. He returned behind the wheel and closed the door.

"What is it?" Stephan asked with trepidation.

Edward took a breath, realizing this was going to be a rather large hit. "It's another picture. They weren't kidding."

"What?" Stephan whimpered.

Edward passed him the photo and Stephan screamed, "They blew her head off!" before collapsing against the car door sobbing.

Waiting for a good minute to pass, Edward gently asked, "Should we go to the police or the party?"

Stephan took in a long breath and exhaled deeply and turned his wet face to stare at him.

Chapter One

WELCOME TO THE SHITSHOW! screamed from a cocktail napkin the host of today's party Marc Monarch placed before me as he mixed one of his deadly vodka lemonades from behind the bar in his home. Tickled, I picked up the napkin for a closer look.

"I can think of a thousand and two occasions this would have come in handy," I giggled.

Marc's emerald green eyes sparkled as he chuckled with a twisted glee, "Fabulous, isn't it?"

"Is it today's theme or a general warning to us all?" I quipped.

"Take it as you will, love," he taunted, sounding like a saucy Olivia de Havilland.

Marc's pretense could flare as though he were an emperor of aristocratic highbrow snobbery. If one didn't know he was a polite, generous, and overall kind and caring person, a stranger could easily misinterpret him as one cold upper crust queen. But beware: never cross him in any way. I have seen this man become the Wicked Witch of the West.

I grinned as he passed me a crystal highball glass literally filled to the brim.

"Thank you," I said, knowing my sobriety just checked its hat at the door.

Marc raised his cocktail and extended it my way over the bar – dribbling the top of his drink. "Cheers!" he smiled.

"Cheers!" I echoed, joining in the dribbly mess of tapping glasses before taking a short sip and another long look around the vastness of the first floor in his Fort Lauderdale mansion.

It was like the lobby of a grand hotel – one enormous room with bright white walls towering thirty feet from white marble flooring to the white coffered ceiling. Running across the back of the house was a hundred feet of open multi-slide glass doors marrying the outdoors to the inside. A long professional chef's kitchen anchored the epicenter with a fifteen-foot island covered in brilliant nautical blue granite countertops providing two sets of prep sinks. Commercial grade stainless-steel appliances beautifully lined the wall behind the island ready for action. This cooking arena commanded a gaze across the house – through floor-to-ceiling windows showcasing the deep outdoor patio running along the Intercoastal – to catch the occasional yacht passing by. It was a panoramic head turner from left to right – no matter where one stood – especially when using the kitchen sink!

A vast conversation and entertainment area with eight nautical blue club chairs and oversized half-moon shaped sofa that could easily seat another dozen people surrounded an incredibly colossal coffee table that was a perfectly sliced chunk of trunk from a banyan tree – all resting upon a 30'x20' red shag rug. In the corner wall of windows, a shiny black grand piano sat dwarfed by an enormous 325-inch wall-sized flatscreen LED TV across the north wall.

The floating oval indoor bar where Marc and I stood sipping our libations was on the opposite side of the room, topped with the same nautical blue granite counter as the kitchen. A dozen tall empty white leather stools circled the saloon awaiting thirsty guests.

Anchoring the real estate next to the bar and adjacent to the entry foyer was a monolithic Pietro Costantini Mid-Century Italian Saks dark dining room table surrounded by eighteen curved Musa chairs covered in soft silver fabric. Soaring above the table were three enormous Luxxu Waterfall Sputnik chandeliers with beautifully handmade ribbed tubes of crystal glass.

And perfectly dotted throughout this incredible home were oversized works of beautiful, colorful art Marc had collected from around the globe. He designed the space to accommodate a hundred guests inside and another hundred on the pool deck. Every little detail he personally selected delivered style and comfort, while giving his guests no reason to want to leave. Ever.

Taking two and a half years to custom-build, his place was a monstrous work of modern beauty. Yes, one could look in any direction with pause to absorb a pictorial worthy of *Better Mansions Digest*.

"I'm happy you came early," Marc gleamed as he walked from behind the bar around to me. "Let's catch up before the barbarians break through the gates."

I chuckled as he led us over to a couple of the club chairs by the football field sofa. Barefoot as always, Marc was nicely styled in oversized Tommy Bahama island wear. He's a short portly man in his late 40s with a buzzed salt and pepper haircut, and physically reminds me of the character actor Charles Durning in *The Sting* – consistently donning a facial expression looking as if he is about to tell one fantastic dirty joke or blow his top in a fit of rage. And though I personally don't see it anymore, down the right side of his neck, arm, and leg, was one long horrific scar from a private jet crash he survived in 2002.

A clink of pans drew my attention as we passed the kitchen where three sous chefs wearing black chef coats were preparing an array of fares for the party. The island was lined with stacks of white plates, flatware caddy's, stacks of folded white napkins, and a dozen food trays and towers filled with all types of meats, cheeses, seafood, vegetables, fruits, and desserts.

We sat looking onto the Hugh Taylor Birch State Park of trees across the Intercoastal, and Marc lifted his glass again to mine. "Cheers!"

This would be the second of a hundred *Cheers!* we would toast today – with one for every refresher and others just because. And there were to be a great many refreshers and just-becauses this day, as there had been in our 15 years of friendship.

"Cheers," I smiled, spilling my drink that was still too full into my *SHITSHOW!* napkin.

We sipped and Marc's eyes burst open. "And to your retirement, my dear."

I smiled as we toasted once again, sipping once again.

"I must say, that as equally happy as I am for your windfall, I am terribly sad to lose you."

Feeling a bit melancholy, I pursed my lips.

"I'm really a bit reminisce," he continued with his eyes welling up. "I will miss our weekly liquid business meetings."

With a smile I shook my head no. "It's been a fun game, Marc. But I'm tired. I've been working eight days a week since I was sixteen. The buyer arrived right on cue. I'm ready to go." I gave him a wink. "We can still do our liquid lunches."

Marc extended his right hand for a comforting squeeze of my forearm with a sad simper. "I hope they paid you a hundred million – a dollar for every sweat and tear."

My eyes lost it and teared up too, and I mentally suffocated any thought of breaking into a good cry. Selling my life's work – the ad agency I built from the ground up – was a life-changing decision. One I was ready to embrace. With a cracked laugh I said, "That would have been nice, but I settled for about half that."

Marc's eyes blew wide open. His jaw dropped in surprise, and he quickly replaced it with a fantastic smile. "In the fifty ballpark?! How fabulous!"

I cocked my head, holding out my glass for an oncoming *Cheers!* Marc again tapped my glass too hard, dribbling more now onto the floor and screamed, "Good for you, Darling!"

We sipped and he asked, "How long is your hand-holding transition commitment?"

"Six months," I replied.

"And the office building?" He continued.

"Closed on it Wednesday. Six point five over ask."

"Marvelous!" Marc toasted again with a hurrah, and we tinked to drink. "It was so wise of you to buy the property in the Great Recession for pennies on the dollar when it went into foreclosure. I should have bought a few more buildings myself. But this is about you, my dear. I'm simply thrilled for your retirement adventures."

"Thank *you*, Marc. It was you ... your business ... your friendship ... that made all this possible."

I tinked his glass again and we drank, again.

"What does your escape plan entail?" he asked.

"I'm going to find a nice little hut away from mankind and finish my book."

Marc's face beamed. "And write about your family funnies?"

"My very own upscale white trash!"

Another tink and drink.

"You have so many hilarious stories to tell ... and you are a fabulous narrator," he said beaming like a proud brother.

I smiled.

"And once you have finished the next bestseller, you will write a book about my parties!"

I continued the grin without saying a word, and drank, noticing an extremely handsome young set of barely legal deeply tanned gym rat brunette twins approach us wearing tightly fitting bright blue dress shorts and matching blue bow ties with no shirts.

Marc carefully gazed them up and down then praised, "Much *much* better! Those oh-so formal uniforms Sandy had you bring are perfect for the country club ... which is where we are *not*."

Marc looked at me. "Gentlemen, this is my dear friend, Winston."

Waving his hand, he added, "Win, this is Brad and Brent. They will be tending the bars for us today. And just so we know who is who, Brad will be hosting in here and Brent will be hosting the tiki bar."

Enjoying the handsome view, I smiled and said hello.

"Win is VIP and will be only served with the Waterford," Marc instructed as he held out his cocktail and tapped the glass with a fingernail. "You will find a small reserve of the crystalware in each of the stations and shall be used for he and I alone. All other guests are to be served with the acrylic glasses."

The twins nodded their understanding.

Then one of the young men cleared his throat. I literally didn't know which twin it was and wouldn't until they were at their assigned stations. Brad or Brent said, "Question. Why are the cooks wearing professional attire and not what we have on?"

I smiled at the logical audacity of his question and immediately looked at Marc to watch his response.

He smiled with a slow blink. "They, my dear young man, are professional chefs. It's what chefs wear. They are back of the house, so to speak. While you, are front of the house. You make people smile by the very sight of you. Bow tie, beauty, and all.

"And with that, you know where everything is, so I'll leave you to it. Thank you."

As they turned to get to work, Marc stopped them with, "And! To show my appreciation for the last-minute costume change, each of you will receive an additional $500 for your services today. Fair enough?"

Boom! The wonder twins activated their supersonic smiles and were two very happy puppies indeed. Whatever contention there may have been about the short shorts was over. And off to their stations they dashed.

Marc leaned into me, blinking slowly. "I must confess but only to you, my dear, that I'm already five sheets to the wind."

Arriving a little after two that afternoon, it was no surprise. Marc was known for his morning brew of vodka bloodies with multiple snorts of cocaine to wake up.

"When is the vote?" I softly asked.

Marc sighed with resignation. "Oh … the board of directors meeting. My family of bloodsuckers. The whole lot is flying down for our annual lambasting on the first."

He paused and looked somewhere outside. It was a good thirty seconds before he continued, "I believe I may follow your lead and exit from all the business bullshit."

I sipped on my drink and listened intently.

"And I'm telling you this because I've decided The Apology Tour is over. That train has stopped, and I have stepped off.

"All my life I have apologized for this or for that. *Inappropriate behavior?* Oh, I'm sorry. *I offended someone?* Oh, I'm sorry. *My sense of humor or entertainment is not for you?* I'm sorry. *You don't like my brutal honesty – professionally or personally?* Again, I'm sorry."

Marc looked at me, trying to focus on my face and eyes.

11

"Well, I tell you my friend, no more. I am sorry'd out. And I break this announcement to you so you will never think I'm rude or just don't give a fuck. I'm simply no longer sorry. Done. End scene."

I placed my hand on his arm with a naughty smirk. "Is this your resignation speech?"

Marc's face lit up, as though a light bulb had just turned on, and he burst into a roaring laugh. He took a breath, held it in, clutched his chest, and looked as if he inhaled an Ah-Ha Moment. Following a long slow exhale, he declared, "I believe it *was*!"

"Are you *ready* to leave the company?" I cautiously asked.

He looked back outside and said with absolute certainty, "I believe I am."

Marc returned his eye contact to me, took a sip, and declared with a different smile I haven't seen him wear in a very long time, "Good riddance to my self-righteous family. I shall pass the baton. And they can shove it up their asses sideways!"

"If this brings you peace, I'm happy for you." I congratulated and raised my glass. "To riddance!"

Energized, he softly tinked my glass with his, and added, "Yes, darling. Cheers to *that*!"

He wiped another tear that welled in his right eye, shifting topics. "My! We are certainly covering all the goodies on the front end of today's soiree.

"Speaking of goodies … you'll be meeting Antonio soon. He's upstairs, still having a bit of jet lag and was pulling himself together before your arrival."

"Your Brazilian rental?"

Yet another different smile came over him. This one appearing naughty.

"The one." His tone of voice suddenly went hot and floozie. "I flew him in from Amsterdam for a little fix. Marc-y needed some rim work."

We laughed.

"Is he residing in The Netherlands now?" I asked, knowing this is one of Marc's regular high-scale hookers whom I've heard far too much about yet never met.

"No. He had a booking with another client. A Dutch politician I believe. But I was fortunate enough to catch him with an opening in his calendar for this week."

Marc leaned in and whispered mischievously, "I must say Antonio is costing me a tidy fortune. He wanted to vacation in Fiji, but I convinced him to come to Fort Lauderdale since today's shindig was on the calendar. He insisted on ten thousand a day plus the use of my corporate jet to fly him in … with a $20,000 sign on. I told him he had to settle for commercial first class. Daddy had to put his foot down at some point."

"It's too bad none of the Miami boys interest you. You'd save a fortune."

"Oh god no! None of those local trashy whores for me, darling. You know I prefer only the internationals."

We laughed until his houseman Sandy approached with an active iPad in hand. He was a short trim man in his forties, with a nicely groomed salty head of hair and beard and took his job very seriously with absolute precision running the household.

"Excuse me, Marc," he politely interrupted.

"Yes, Sandy," Marc replied.

"A quick update. Steve and Stephen will be landing at the Executive Airport on the company jet in roughly thirty-six minutes. Their ETA to the manor should be in about an hour.

"Today we have six service personnel who will be cleaning areas, washing collected serve ware, and restocking food and drink stations.

"Mayor Grayson and Commissioner Daniels will not be able to attend and send their regards."

"Thank you, Sandy," Marc smiled, adding, "Oh, our two bartenders have different uniforms and will be receiving an additional $500 per ... *if* they work the party start to finish."

"Yes, sir," Sandy confirmed.

"Hello, Mr. Clarke," Sandy smiled with a polite nod.

"Hi, Sandy," I greeted, and he was off.

"Well, toodles!" Marc said rather annoyed.

I watched him think but said nothing.

He looked at me and vented, "I sent half the company's security team, along with S&S, to a national security conference in Denver this past week."

Steve and Steven, Marc's personal security guys – who he called S&S for short simplicity – I'd met and had been given Marc's VIP status that cleared me to come and go as I liked.

Marc continued. "When an early blizzard hit Colorado on Thursday, the entire team couldn't fly out until this morning. S&S were slated to be here for the party to check people in at the door. And *they're* the ones arriving fashionably late."

He took a breath. The reality was what it was, and added, "Okie Dookie then."

Another thought struck him, and he spontaneously glanced to his left at the monster back wall TV and uttered with surprise to himself, "Heavens-to-Betsy ... final touches! Focus!"

He pulled out a cell phone from his shorts pocket, tapped a few times, and *BAM!* an enormous Celine Dion was in concert across the north end with audio blasting at high volume everywhere – startling us, and undoubtedly everyone inside and out.

"Oopsie!" Marc yelped and quickly lowered the sound to a suitable level.

"The last time I had this on I was having a party of one," he tittered and followed my glance back to the TV.

"This is her *That's Just the Woman in Me* special."

We watched the dancers bounce around Ms. Dion for a minute until Marc turned to me and cooed, "She *is* absolutely breathtaking."

I smiled, cuing his next round of *Cheers!* Another tink, another drink, and Marc glanced over to the foyer and popped, "Ah! Tom and Jerry are here."

He turned to me and declared in a soft glib tone, "Why are next door neighbors always the first to arrive and last to leave?"

"How many are on the guest list?" I asked.

As Marc slowly made his girthy way off the chair and to a vertical stance, he grunted, "Half the Marys in Broward County will be mincing and prancing their way onto the premises any minute. Far too many without an RSVP, no doubt. And with S&S running late, the uninvited tally will be something special, I'm sure."

He focused on me, and then on my glass and chirped, "My god, darling! You're half empty!"

With that, he grabbed the glass from my hand, slopping an ice cube onto the floor, and moseyed to the bar. "Time for refills!"

"Refills?!" Tom shrieked from afar, pulling out a seat at the bar.

I stood and followed Marc … amused by his slumbering walk which was more of a squiggle than a straight line. I glanced at Tom and Jerry – the tall and skinny seasoned duo whose hairdos were identical and outfits always color coordinated as if they're about to jump off the cover of a fashion magazine.

"Honey, it looks like we missed the first pour!" Jerry – who is forever donning a Cheshire cat grin – greeted Marc with a hug.

Tom shifted from the bar stool and went in to hug our host. And out of nowhere, he threw his hands in the air as if he's going for a cheerleader High V, and yelled, "Touchdown for us!"

"For Christ's sakes Susie, you're sixty-two years old … put away the pom poms!" Marc gaffed as he handed Brad the glasses and asked him for another round of vodka lemonades.

Okay, Brad is inside, and Brent is *outside* my mind noted.

"And how exactly did you get a touchdown out of that?" Mark sniped.

"He's sixty-*three* and easily excitable!" Jerry slung.

Tom violently gasped.

"Did you just *gasp*?" Jerry sarcastically dropped.

"I most certainly did," Tom snapped.

Jerry retorted, "I thought you got a prescription for that."

"You know my retched little precious, for our twenty-fifth anniversary, I believe I'll pick up a big uncooked ham and roll of duct tape, and we'll go for a long drive into the Everglades … where the alligators love to dine." Tom spat.

Jerry covered his mouth with his fingertips and in a high-pitch childlike voice squealed sarcastically, "Oooh … I'm in *danger*!"

"Girls! Girls! Girls!" Marc commanded. "Let's save the Chip and Dale chipmunk schtick until there's a full house!"

Before I said a word, oversized pals Keith and Rafael entered. They spotted Tom and Jerry, and cautiously examined what they were walking in to. Keith, in his late sixties, was a man not concerned about his fitness or trim whatsoever. Rafael was a fifty-something round man like Keith, though very well could

16

have been the twin brother of the interior designer character Otho in the original movie *Beetlejuice*.

"Lookie who were just rolled off the beach by good Samaritans and brought in out of the sun!" Jerry said all too flippantly.

Tom added, "I'd say your house is full now, Marc."

"Tom. Jerry," is all Keith said in a cold polite greeting as he gave Marc a hug.

Rafael went in for his friendly embrace then looked into Marc's eyes and said rather high-browed with all seriousness, "I promise I'll be on my best behavior today." He abruptly snapped his head and fat neck for a direct stare down at Tom and Jerry. "But I also see you have a rodent infestation. If there's any RatX in the house, it will be my pleasure to rid these pesky squirrels for you, Marc."

Tom and Jerry's jaws fell in unison.

Marc turned and looked at me with an exasperated smirk that screamed, "For fuck's sake!"

Far too sober to dance with this loud obnoxious gaggle before the festivities began, I slid my hand into the left side pocket of my khaki cargo shorts to reach for my cigarette case – preparing for a quick getaway outdoors. "Hello, gentlemen," I finally greeted.

"Win!" The four professional adversaries shouted as if I were Norm on *Cheers* – though not with the same 'thrilled to see you, welcome back' acclaim … more like *'And then there's Maude'* bellow.

None of us socialized outside the LGBT curriculum circuit. We only saw one another at fundraising events and galas, or groundbreaking ceremonies for nonprofit centers assisting and treating those in need of food, shelter, medical assistance or medications, or award presentations celebrating the top philanthropic individuals in our community each year, or the theater, or Marc's parties.

Socially, I've never been considered *unapproachable* ... simply *distant*. And with this distance, for many in gay society gossip, I am considered *too private* or *too cold* or *too frigid* – especially if I didn't know someone, or dare I say, find someone unreal, untrustworthy, or unlikable.

Professionally, the reality was my bandwidth was channeled entirely on work. The pressures of spearheading one of the largest ad agencies in South Florida took tremendous concentration to ensure everything all the time was smooth sailing for the ninety-three associates at Winston Clarke. I was in a league of my own. Actually, I was alone running a league. That is, until Wednesday when I also signed papers that sold my associates to the highest bidder.

So, there were no honest or pretend hugs with the first batch of arrivals – which was perfectly fine with us all. I was Marc's friend, and they were Marc's friends. Somewhat strangers in life but friendly in these social situations. My status was always the kind harmless outsider who many were polite with. And as these four would gnaw on one another all day long, I was left unbitten.

*   *   *

There was a time a couple decades ago, when Tom, Jerry, Keith and Rafael were positively the best of friends. And real. And trustworthy. And likable.

These four pals collectively decided one summer evening over happy hour commiserations at a gay bar in Wilton Manors, they were all unsatisfied with their careers and decided to get their real

18

estate licenses together and go into business buying and flipping houses in dilapidated neighborhoods – creating new gayborhoods. And that, they did.

Between 2003 and 2007, as the housing market exploded in South Florida, these four highly driven men soon realized the flipping side of the business was better placed on hold as they listed and sold homes faster than they could ever imagine. In those four years, their small agency sold more than a billion dollars' worth of residential properties.

In '08, when the bottom of the housing gold rush fell out and they found themselves spending more time together in their office, Tom and Jerry swiftly grew tired of Keith and Rafael's gruff demeanors ... while Keith and Rafael realized they no longer enjoyed the Tom and Jerry Banter Act. By the next year, they mutually agreed to dissolve their boutique agency and bitterly go their separate ways before the office became a blood splatter crime scene.

Today, all four men work part time competing for the occasional $2-10 million dollar listing ... with Team 1 intensely loathing Team 2, and vice versa.

*   *   *

Brad set Marc's requested refills on the bar as the two chopsticks and two sushi rolls began ordering drinks over one another.

I stepped into Marc's glossy gaze, leaned in, and asked gently, "Are you alright?"

He snapped back to reality with a smile, reached for our drinks and handed me mine. "Settle in, darling. I'm going to the ladies' room for a minute."

Knowing this was Marc's code for his fix, I whispered with a smile, "Go powder your nose."

"You must share one of your fabulous family funnies when I return."

"Absolutely," I smiled, wondering how long my friend would be vertical for his own party.

Pleased, he nodded and turned to Tom, Jerry, Rafael, and Keith as if to say something like, "Play nice, you animals!" But knowing it would have been wasted words, he simply headed for the elevator off the foyer.

Pulling a fag from my cigarette case and lifting for everyone to see, I asked, "Smoke anyone?"

Of course, no one did. They all used to years ago. But no longer. This habit that was once theirs had been kicked to the curb. And in its place was born an absolute disdain for tobacco smokers.

Ignoring the few glares fired my way, I pulled the Ray-Bans from my shirt collar, slid them on, and happily made my exit. With a properly filled drink in hand, I was relieved this vodka lemonade wouldn't become a splish or splash balancing act.

Stepping through the open wall outside, it was a perfect 72 degrees on this sunny second Saturday in October. Firing up my cigarette, I walked across the enormous outdoor patio that was nothing short of perfection – trimmed with all the best decorating goodies a summertime *Frontgate* catalog could offer. A gigantic pool with a side jacuzzi ran parallel to the Intercoastal as medium and large yachts cruised by. And here and there were cozy seating areas with teak chairs dressed in clean white cushions surrounding round teak tables centered with glass fire pits.

Making my way to the edge of the patio deck where an enormous marine blue umbrella shaded another seating area

Marc designated as *the only* smoking area on the grounds, I walked past the covered tiki hut bar that could seat six – nodded a smile to Brent as he continued to set up his station – and strolled to my usual seat along the seawall. I sat. It was the perfect spot with a clear view of the house, pool, waterway, and sheer tranquility that would be all mine – for at least the next few minutes.

I glanced at the six crystal ashtrays placed around the table before every chair and puffed on my smoke, grinning over the first time I mentioned the outdoor accessories to Marc.

"Darling, you can't imagine the thousands of dollars I've spent on designer crystal ashtrays to fill my apartments in Manhattan, London, Barcelona, and Singapore," he replied.

"When the world decided indoor smoking was taboo, I was left with dozens of these things that had no purpose. Until I decided *who says crystal cannot be poolside*?! So please, ash your butt in only the finest money can buy!"

I rested my drink on a slate coaster and gazed to the left of the entryway at an outdoor grilling station where two more sous chefs were busy setting up the BBQ with four tables nicely covered in white linens topped with more stacks of white plates and cloth napkins, flatware towers, and buffet chafing pans. And to my far left between the tiki bar and Intercoastal, was a long dining tent that could seat seventy-five people comfortably beneath lighted running ceiling fans.

Smoking away, enjoying the serenity, I thought on what Marc said about the end of his apology tour speech to his family of moguls. And his resigning as Chairman versus being voted out of the family business with disgrace.

These were huge steps for someone who inherited a billion-dollar family-owned empire. Yet here Marc was – standing on the edge of a comfortable nest he'd never left – with *the* decision to either jump or get pushed out. I was honestly surprised he was ready to take that leap.

All of a sudden out of nowhere, I had a strong strange feeling this could very well be my last visit, here … *at Marc's place.*

Chapter Two

Marc Monarch and I first met at the members-only club Twenty-8 in downtown Fort Lauderdale one rainy afternoon in 2009. My office was two blocks from the 28th floor restaurant bar boasting 360-degree views of the city, the Atlantic Ocean, Miami, and the Everglades. Always a visually relaxing spot, I'd pop in for a bite and clear my head for new advertising ideas to brew.

On this fateful day, I strolled into the building for a drink to celebrate my landing another auto dealership group's advertising account seconds before the skies opened with a heavy downpour. *More green lights!* My mind happily praised with gratitude as I strode into an open elevator ready to serve.

Twenty-eighth floor. The elevator halted and announced. Stepping off, I walked into a lounge where the usual high-rise views were now canvassed with low-hanging black clouds rolling by every window – an ominous yet exciting visual to be surrounded by. It was the perfect vibe to applaud my success in solidarity.

I saw a short portly gentleman with dark hair sitting at the bar whom I've seen at the club on occasion, but never had the pleasure of formally meeting. It was also the first time I noticed a pink scar on the side of his neck that ran into hiding beneath his long-sleeved Maus & Hoffman tailored shirt.

Pulling out a tall stool covered in black tufted leather two places away from him at the bar, I took my seat and was welcomed by Lisa, the daytime barkeep who forever wore the most infectious smile. "Good afternoon, Winston," she always greeted and instantly poured my forever go to – Gentlemen's Jack on the rocks – unless I'd change things up with something different by request. Once she placed my beverage before me, he spoke.

"What a strikingly powerful name you have," cooed the stranger with incredibly glowing green eyes.

Raising my glass, I thanked him with a smile. This not highly attractive nor unattractive fellow raised his glass, leaned over for a *Cheers!* and we cocktail tapped.

"I'm Marcus," he added, reaching his hand out for a shake. "But call me Marc with a 'c'."

"A pleasure to meet you, Marc with a 'c'." I grinned and shook his hand, feeling as though I knew this person somehow. But where?

"Mr. Monarch," Lisa politely acknowledged as she replaced his drink that was a half inch from empty.

"Thank you, Lisa," he replied softly, then looked at me as he sipped.

"What brings you in to this slice of heaven so high in the sky?" He asked.

"A new client signed on today," I smiled, feeling quite proud of this victory that took two years to land. "Time to celebrate."

Marc stared at me in concentrated thought for a moment. "You wouldn't happen to be the Winston of Winston Clarke & Associates on the building across the street, would you?"

I grinned. "At your service."

"Yes, Winston Clarke," Marc confirmed. "What do your associates do, Winston?"

"Call me Win," I said, sipped my drink, then answered, "Advertising."

The stranger burst into a hearty laugh. A flash of lightning and thunderous crack boomed the building. The club's lights flickered but stayed on.

"Destiny has arrived!" Marc wailed with an enormous smile of excitement.

I sipped again, curious why this would be so incredibly amusing to a man I just met.

He shook his head and collected himself. Marc gulped his drink and turned to say, "Life is filled with ironies."

"Yes," I smiled in agreement.

He glanced out one of the sky windows catching more lightning firing off. His demeanor shifted, as though something had triggered an idea. Marc's green eyes return to mine. Then suddenly, he broke from a look of processing which of a thousand questions to begin with, to a friendly smile that confirmed he was back in the present.

"Where are your roots?" he asked. "Your dialect has a hint of middle America."

"I grew up in a small-town north of Fort Wayne, Indiana, in the land of corn and soybeans and farms and Amish."

"A Hoosier!" he smiled with approval.

"And you?" I asked.

"Wisconsin," Marc smiled. "The land of cheese and greeting cards."

That's it! My mind rang. This is Marc Monarch, CEO and Chairman of Monarch Global – the greeting card and cable television network empire. I read in *South Florida Business People* magazine he recently moved his corporate office from Madison, Wisconsin, to Fort Lauderdale.

"To we Midwesterners," I held my glass out for another toast.

Marc smiled widely, our cocktails tapped, and we sipped. A desire for a cigarette was kicking in and I began to think of a quick dash down to the parking garage for a smoke, since my usual spot on the open-air rooftop patio with no overhead covering was currently being drenched by downpour.

"The next round is on me," Marc declared with an air there was more than another round that was on him.

That rainy afternoon, the club was light on members. We had the entire bar to ourselves. Something told me to hold off on the nicotine fix because *something* was about to happen here.

Marc Monarch and I drank and talked about the unique blend of people in Fort Lauderdale – how it was more international with a flux of New Yorkers versus the West Coast of Florida where the tourists and locals were mostly from the Midwest. We talked about how traditional advertising in print, radio and television was changing as we moved into the 2010s, and how the internet would one day be a primary arena of promotion.

As another series of lightning flashed and boomed around us on the 28th floor, Marc and I moved to a sitting area with club chairs to lounge and chat more comfortably. Strangely, our newfound friendship felt very easy. The more we spontaneously began sharing our lives, the more it felt like we'd been the best of friends since primary school and hadn't seen one another in thirty years.

"May I ask you a personal question?" He asked.

"Please," I replied.

"Husband?"

"Widower."

Marc clutched his chest with a small gasp, somewhat embarrassed.

To quickly shift gears, I assured, "It is a love story with a Shakespearian ending I'll share over drinks another time."

Reading the cue, Marc smiled in agreement and followed my lead. "I'd like that," he said. And without skipping a beat, bypassing any potential long awkward silence, Marc asked, "Shall I share a little about my story?"

"Please," I smiled. Curious. And rather relieved.

*　　*　　*

The *Thank You Note* company his great great great grandmother Ibby Monarch conceived in the fall of 1870 in Madison, Wisconsin, had grown into a global brand by turn of the century. The wife a successful cheese maker, Ibby became unsatisfied handwriting long thank you notes to all the hosts of high-society parties she and her husband attended. She felt if there were a selection of lovely note cards, each with a different butterfly – after the Monarch name – painted on the cover with a *Thank You* pre-inked inside, all she would have to do is simply sign *All Our Best, Ibby & Charles* and be done with it.

Ibby hired a local artist, Helen Littlejohn, to hand paint fifty different monarch butterfly scenes on the outside of folding notes made of heavy parchment. The day a box of the scenic cards was personally delivered by the elderly Scottish woman who created the works of art with her old wrinkly hands, Ibby carefully placed them neatly side by side across her long dining room table for a view alongside Helen.

The more Ibby savored the artistic beauty on each of these individual works of art, the more perplexed she became. These were too pretty to simply give away, she thought. And in one social season, she would use each and every one.

Ibby said nothing of her consternation to her artist, rather, politely asking, "May I hire you to paint five more of each of these – identical to the originals you brought today?"

Helen answered with a nod, "Yes, Mi Lady."

Barely able to contain the ideas of commercializing these in her head, Ibby smiled. "Wonderful. And I would like one additional set of each on fine white stock you would use for a display in a gallery."

Mrs. Monarch walked over to her small secretary desk in the next room, pulled a check ledger from a drawer, and placed it gently on the desktop. She took a step back to look through the wooden arched walkway to Helen who remained in the dining room gathering up her display of cards to take home and replicate perfectly. "Please," Ibby waved to the small parlor sofa beside her desk, "join me."

Helen walked in and took a seat. Ibby sat at her desk with a smile. "How much of your time did each one of these beautiful pieces take to paint?"

"Roughly a half hour," Helen replied.

Ibby calculated in her mind it took Helen roughly twenty-five hours to paint these fifty cards.

"How did you come up with so many different scenes with the monarch butterflies?" Ibby asked.

"I looked out the window." Helen smiled.

Rather confused, Ibby didn't understand how that was possible. "It's February."

Helen replied, "I used memories."

Highly impressed with Helen's visual recall she paused for a long smile and said, "We agreed upon fifty cents per card, correct?"

"Yes, Mi Lady."

"And we agreed this would be in confidence, correct?"

"We did. And it is."

Ibby smiled and turned to her desk to reach for a small sheet of paper. She wrote several mathematical equations with a pencil, underlining a final number once she was done.

"For all your materials, and paints, and brushes, and time and beautiful talents, do you feel five-hundred dollars is a fair price for what you presented today and to complete my next order?"

This was an extraordinary amount of money! Helen Littlejohn gulped. And nodded carefully not to expose her jubilance.

Ibby smiled in agreement. She turned to her check registry, reached for her writing quill to dip in ink and wrote two two-hundred and fifty dollar checks payable to Helen Littlejohn. She pulled a long parchment envelope from a lower desk drawer on her left, refreshed the quill with ink, and wrote Helen's full name in beautiful calligraphy across its face. She blew upon one check to ensure the ink was dry and slid it inside.

"I would like the identical five paintings separated and bundled together, so there are fifty individual sets," Ibby instructed.

"Of course, Mi Lady," Helen confirmed.

Ibby handed Helen a check. "Two installments. Half now. Half upon the next delivery."

"Of course, Mi Lady," Helen said realizing she was repeating herself.

Ibby held the envelope up to show Helen, before placing it between two books on the shelf above her desk. "I will be traveling abroad soon. And if I'm not here for your next delivery, this is where your second installment is. Be sure to let our house lady, Mrs. Miller, know to give this to you if I'm away."

The two ladies smiled in gratitude for one another. The money couldn't have come at a better time for Mrs. Littlejohn. And Mrs.

Monarch was already seeing herself in Chicago calling upon printers specializing in Chromoxylography.

*   *   *

"In that special moment of time, The Monarch Card Company was born," Marc Monarch explained in the second hour of our first meeting.

As Lisa delivered another round of drinks and cleaned our little area, I couldn't help but inquire, "What prompted your corporate relo to Fort Lauderdale?"

Mr. Monarch laughed, "Wisconsin winters, darling!"

I nodded in agreement, not missing the snow either.

Surprisingly, I felt Marc was studying me ... wanting to say something, as he had within moments of my arrival.

"Tell me about your family growing up," he came out and asked.

With a sip, I decided to make it short and sweet. "Mother was from rural Indiana, went to Chicago for her education and became a teacher. Father grew up in Fort Wayne and became an architect. After they married, years were spent trying to conceive a child. Mother finally became pregnant, carried to near term, and had a stillborn. A year later they adopted me. Three years after, mother again was pregnant, and *again* carried to near term to have another stillborn. The following year, they adopted my sister.

"Father built a beautiful home on a lake north of Fort Wayne in Mother's hometown of Hicksville. We were the perfect upper middle class American family with Mother becoming manic depressive once sis arrived, and Father, as the wonderful provider he was, became an alcoholic to cope with Mother.

30

"They eventually divorced. Father remarried and created a *Brady Bunch* integration. Mother became a mad hoarder.

"And now, after all we children have grown, my family is a tribe of toleration."

Marc sat quietly and slowly blinked. I sipped my drink. *A cigarette about now sounds really really good!* my mind rang.

"You must have quite the bankroll of family stories," he finally said.

I smiled. "I do."

Curious, he crossed his legs and leaned in my direction. "You mentioned your mother was manic depressive. I don't know what exactly that is. May I ask you to share an example of your experience with your mother's illness?"

"Of course. Let me preface," I began, "I am perfectly comfortable sharing how my mind has captured the comedy from the scarring. And with that, I value these shockingly funny moments in my life as brilliant comedic wisdom … so it's okay to laugh."

Highly intrigued, Marc smiles. "Okay…"

"Are you ready?"

"Yes."

"Are you sure?" I confirmed.

"Of course," Marc snapped with a bit of impatience that I punched too much into the lead.

"Growing up, there were always some weird behavioral oddities my mother would exhibit that I didn't understand. Through her conditioning with me as a child, I learned early on if Mother would scream and end up on the floor, that was *bad*.

"When a child grows up in an environment where *anything* can trigger *bad*, then one generally tries to be on their best

31

behavior … or immediately do whatever possible to fix *the bad* right away. It's a hopping on eggshells kind of syndrome.

"In this story, I was four or five and accidentally spilled a full glass of milk on the kitchen table. It was flowing everywhere and found the shortest point to the edge, where a stream began to run onto the linoleum floor.

"I'm all by myself but quickly realized if I cleaned it up fast, *it never happened.*

"Mother was taking a nap or passed out or something, and I had plenty of time. Or so I thought.

"I dashed over to the hanging roll of paper towels above the dishwasher and with a long yank – and I'm thinking five or six feet should do the trick – I ripped it off in one hefty tug and spun around to get back to the kitchen table in a hurry … and there's Mother … standing at the end of the table with her eyes exploding open in horror. She's in a frozen spooked cat lockdown stance. Suddenly, she slapped the sides of her face with hands clenched, like a 50s B-movie queen who just ran into the Creature from the Black Lagoon and belted out a horrific murder scream.

"I stood in disbelief.

"'WHY WINSTON! OH, WINSTON, WHY?!' She moaned in revulsion as if I had done something God awful.

"'DON'T YOU EVER DO THAT TO A ROLL OF PAPER TOWELS!' Mother shrieked … before dropping to the floor in absolute shock."

Marc's belly jiggled as he giggled. "Oh, shit!" was all he could muster. Covering his mouth with a hand, his eyes began to water as he broke into a heartier laugh.

I watched him in amazement, wondering why this was doing him in. It was after all, a very short story. Yet here was this man splitting apart.

Barely able, he choked out, "What did Mother do *then*?"

"She sobbed," I replied matter of fact. "A good half hour cry."

He buckled. "*Over paper towels?*" was all he could utter.

Marc collapsed backward into the club chair and began to stomp his feet as if his body was physically pleading for oxygen. He would have slid out had he not been clutching its arms for dear life to remain seated.

Mr. Monarch waved his hands as if to say something. "It's … it's *the visual* …" he choked out, mimicking clenched fists tapping his cheeks.

I glanced at Lisa who stood alone at the bar, and gathered, between the volume in which I emulated *Mother's Paper Towel Fright* and Marc's laughing yelps, she heard it all. We locked into a moment of eye contact. And with an expression of someone caught giggling, she nodded with a smile and pretended to go back to work doing something else.

The volume of my drunken tale must have been excessive, I realized, and finally decided I could no longer hold off a smoke.

As my new friend continued to roar beside me, two businessmen entered from an elevator, each carrying large wet umbrellas, ready for their happy hour.

"Marc, please excuse me for a moment," I said. "I'll be right back."

He waved me off, laugh-crying his goodness graciousness.

I dashed over to the garage express elevator and zipped down for a quick smoke of half a cigarette. Returning to the club level, I darted into the men's room to wash my hands, popped a mint in my mouth, and swiftly returned to Marc's side. A new round of drinks was delivered while I was away, and the billionaire appeared to have returned to a level of calm bliss.

"I must thank you, Mr. Clarke," he said. "That was a fabulous story. Thank you."

I picked up my drink and welcomed him.

"I see from where your creativity generates and why you've chosen the world of advertising as a profession," he now spoke in a serious manner sounding composed. "You are a humble man, Winston. You're honest. Forthright. Have zero pretense. All qualities I find admirable."

Why did I suddenly feel as though I were on a job interview? I wondered and smiled. "Thank you."

Marc took a deep breath as though he was mentally confirming what he was about to say. And then he spoke. "I have a new product I'm developing. It's a different type of card that has not been done, and I am rather confident there's an enormous untapped market."

He paused for a long sip of his fresh drink. "I'm going to share the highly confidential details and I would like you to give me a pitch on what the brand should be called."

Not seeing this direction coming, I took a long sip from my drink too. Marc looked around to ensure we are far enough away from anyone. His voice lowered and softened to a loud whisper.

"It's *I Hate You* cards to send to one's enemy or frenemy. The series includes *I'm Calling You Out* cards and *You Are A Horrible Human* cards."

Stunned, I sipped again. This was one incredible idea or one horrific idea. I wasn't sure what to think.

"So, Mr. Winston Clarke and Associates," Marc began to slur, "you have five minutes to sell me a name for this brand of note card. And the account is yours."

We both sipped again and stared into each other's eyes.

Marc looked at his watch fuzzily, then shouted, "And, GO!"

Another flash of lightning filled the 28th floor followed by another crackling boom.

Feeling as though I was in a final round of *Jeopardy!* and the countdown music began to play, my mind began to race.

I Hate You cards.
You Are A Horrible Human notes.
What the fuck would these be called?

I stood and walked over to Lisa at the bar for a pen and handful of white beverage napkins to scribble on as thoughts picked up speed.

This is a rather sick and twisted product line!
Who would buy these things?
Bitter people would.
Angry people would.
Spiteful people would.
Yes – this was an untapped market!

Three more members arrived and ponied up to the bar for her greetings.

The clock is ticking! I heard scream within as my gaze watched the newcomers with a mentally focused blank stare.

And then the million-dollar brand name came. I wrote it down. Double checked it. I double double checked it. "That's it!" I proudly said to myself with ratification.

Returning to my seat beside Marc, I handed him the bev nap. He smiled, never taking his eyes off mine for what seemed like a rather long time. He looked at my scribble. And stared at my scribble. And kept staring at my scribble.

I drank my cocktail down like it was a glass of water.

Finally, Marc Monarch folded the napkin and tucked it in his shirt pocket. He gulped his drink dry and turned to Lisa holding the glass in the air. He returned to me to say calmly and without emotion, "I mentioned earlier that destiny had arrived. And the reason I made that declaration is, not ten minutes before you walked in, I decided to not renew our ad agency's contract, which expires in six weeks. I have spent the past four months reviewing dozens of RFPs from top agencies around the planet who wants my business. And not one of the Request for Proposals have come close to what you just did with two words on a cocktail napkin in less than five minutes.

"Today is a very successful day for you," he continued, "I would like to congratulate your agency landing Arthur Automotive Group with dealerships throughout Broward and Miami-Dade Counties. And I would like to formally offer Winston Clarke & Associates a contract to be the new agency-of-record for Monarch Global – with a $50 million annual advertising budget."

This stranger three hours ago, held out his hand once again. My entire body shook with adrenalin in that handshake.

Lisa returned with fresh drinks in the nick of time.

Marc picked up the new cocktail and raised his glass for a toast. "Cheers!"

We tapped.

"Thank you," I smiled and softly echoed, "Cheers."

Love Nōts

Several weeks later, again at Twenty-8 over drinks with the Monarch Global/WC&A contracts signed, Marc felt it was important I know more about the history of the Monarchs and shared his family tree.

"Two worthy mentions up front on the Monarch family lineage," he began.

"Since my great great great grandmother Ibby, there has been this repetitive need to name ourselves after ourselves. One example, my younger sister was named five generations later, after Ibby.

"And great great great grandfather Marcus – whom I'll address as Marcus since he was the first of six generational Marcus's to carry the name. I'm the sixth. So, I will number every generation of Marcus's like M2, M3, M4.

"Because Lordie … I can repeat my own name so many times before I'm on my last gay nerve. Understand?"

I nodded yes and drank and listened.

"Ibby's family were dairy farmers who were very successful in the Madison, Wisconsin, region in the mid-1800s.

"Marcus's family were cheesemakers who bought their dairy products from Ibby's parents.

"Ibby and Marcus knew one another their entire lives. And though Marcus was ten years her senior, Ibby had always been rather smitten with him. But Marcus was busy with higher education then worked for the family business alongside his brothers Charles and Chester.

"It wasn't until Ibby's Coming Out Ball for her sixteenth birthday, that Marcus actually took notice of Ibby's beauty as a young woman. He was besotted. And they married a year later, the day after her graduation from primary school.

"A progressive duo, Ibby and Marcus, chose to travel the world twice a year during their first three years of marriage, having decided to hold off on children until Ibby graduated from a women's college the following year. However, her drive for card making changed the course of her higher education – which was a rarity for women at that time.

"It was May of 1871 when Ibby filed her Articles of Incorporation with the State of Wisconsin to launch her small business with Marcus's blessing. He adored her brilliant idea and entrepreneurial spirit and encouraged his young wife every step of the way. She made many trips to Chicago to custom print her cards and matching envelopes. And on September 1st, Ibby opened her first store in downtown Madison called The Monarch Thank You Note Card Company.

"While the year was busy for Ibby, it was also an exciting one for Marcus who was developing new cheeses for a growing market of high-end consumers looking for fancier food items called *gourmet*.

"One of the new products Marcus created and test-marketed successfully was a maple syrup white cheddar that had become a favorite in the cheese baskets he and Ibby would bring to dinner parties, attended by other successful business families in Madison. At one such event, it was suggested to Marcus he travel to a small town called Peshitgo, about a hundred and fifty miles north, where there were plenty of maple tree farmers he could negotiate a better price on the syrup than what he had been paying the local distributors in Madison.

"Three weeks after the opening of Ibby's card shoppe, it was decided he would travel to Peshtigo the first week of October while the Indian Summer remained warm and dry. His brother Charles also planned a trip to Chicago for the same week to meet several distributors and introduce their new lines of gourmet cheeses to sell throughout Illinois. Youngest brother Chester remained home with his father to run the operations.

"On October 7, both men boarded trains – Marcus heading northeast and Charles heading southeast. Little did either know, it would be the last time they would kiss their wives goodbye or see one another again.

"For, October 8, 1871, was a fateful Sunday night for both these men. The Great Chicago Fire erupted and destroyed more than 3 square miles of the city. And in a horrific twist of fate, the Peshtigo Fire erupted at exactly the same time and burned over 1.1 million acres in a firestorm fueled by strong winds blowing in from the west.

"Great great great grandfather Marcus perished that night with 2,400 other souls, as did my great great great uncle Charles with 300 souls.

"A month later, widow Ibby discovered she was a pregnant with child.

"The following year, Marcus II – M2 – arrived and Ibby made the decision not to sell her deceased husband's shares in The Creamy Cheese Company back to the family. She also chose not to involve herself with the affairs of its operations. Rather, she would focus her future on raising her two children: her son and her thank you note company. The family cheese business would continue to be run by her father-in-law and Chester, and the monthly dividends received for her shares would maintain financial comfort as she moved forward with life.

"By 1892, M2 had grown into a young man working alongside his mother and The Monarch Thank You Note Card Company blossomed with new stores in Chicago, St. Louis, New York City, Atlanta, Louisville, and Denver.

"While on a trip to St. Louis, he met his future wife Marjorie, and they had two children -- Marcus III and Esther. He built his new family a lovely Victorian Home in a neighborhood close to his mother. Once they were all settled in, M2, began a zig-zag tour across the country introducing the Monarch brand to the fastest growing cities.

"The first week of September in 1900, M2 was covering the Dallas/Houston markets, and decided to travel south to Galveston for some fishing over the weekend before catching a train back home the following week to see his wife and young children.

"No one saw it coming, and when the Great Galveston Hurricane of 1900 arrived on September 8, it took M2's life with 8,000 souls.

"M3 and Esther grew up fatherless but were loved more than anything by their adoring mother Marjorie. M3 joined the family business working alongside his grandmother Ibby. And sadly, days before her eighteenth birthday, Esther fell ill to the Spanish Flu and died.

"Two months later, Marjorie died of a broken heart from the loss of her baby girl.

"By 1919, the family bloodline consisted of only Ibby and M3, who was now twenty-two. A hardworking man, M3 preferred the professional excitement of his grandmother's company versus a higher education at Yale or Harvard. He wanted to stay in Madison, in all reality, because he had fallen in love with a young socialite named Elizabeth. And though Ibby wanted her grandson to attain the knowledge and experiences from an Ivy League college, she was relieved when he had a frank discussion about how he saw his future with her, running the company side by side, and not wasting time with fraternal follies.

"Ibby rewarded M3 by promoting him to president and he and Elizabeth were married in 1920 and had four lovely children – Esther the second, Sarah, Mary, and M4.

"Over the next decade, the Monarch business expanded into an international brand by opening stores in Ontario, Quebec, and Montreal. And though the Great Depression hit the country hard, Ibby made national headlines as a generous businesswoman who provided a cup of hot soup to anyone hungry at each of the Monarch stores across the country for the entire year of 1931.

"Ibby died in 1933 at the feisty age of eighty-two.

"M3's children grew seemingly all too quickly, and before he knew it, M4 had grown and was in love with a beautiful lady named Theresa. They married on September 1, 1945, the day before the end of World War II.

"M4 and Theresa had two children, Oakaline and M5.

"M3 died of a heart attack in 1950, and M4 was immediately moved into his father's position as president and CEO.

"Oakaline and her Aunt Mary were killed in a boating accident in 1960, when a drunken boater sped across Lake Mendota at dusk without his boat lights on, and little Oakaline who was fourteen and driving the boat, didn't react in time and they collided in the middle of the lake. All three drowned.

"M5 grew up and married a young woman named Julianne in 1964. They had four children – me, Ibby Two, Esther the third, and Marjorie the second – we called her Maggie.

"Mother took Esther and Maggie on a trip to visit her cousin Turnip in Big Thompson Canyon in Colorado during the summer of 1976. Their travels coincided at the exact moment a flash flood with a wall of water more than twenty feet high swept through

Big Thompson Canyon – taking my mother and Maggie, along with 143 souls on July 31st. Esther was washed away and miraculously lived!

"In '95, during a winter blizzard, my father and grandfather – M4 and M5 – were driving home from a business trip to Milwaukee when a semi blew a tire and veered into their car head on. Its trailer was a carrying a large tank of gasoline, and well … a fiery end right there right then.

"So now, it's me, my sister Esther who still wishes she died in the flood with mother, and sister Ibby Two, who wishes I were dead. Ibby Two's four hooligans she calls her children, along with Esther's two misfits, all want control of the company.

"That's my family tree," Marc said before gulping another freshly poured cocktail from Lisa.

Sweet Mother Mary of God! I thought but said, "That's a six-part Monarch TV movie of the week or mini-series, Marc."

"It certainly would be … if it were *anyone else's* family," he grinned.

*   *   *

One of the first bold moves Marc Monarch made when stepping into the shoes of his father and grandfather in taking over Monarch Greeting Cards in 1995, was change its name to just Monarch. "Everyone in the world knows what a Monarch greeting card is. Why be redundant?" He'd say – not ask.

By 1997, the rebranding of Monarch was completed for its butterfly gift products – including greeting cards, keepsake ornaments, stationary, books, picture frames, bookmarks, and holiday decorations. A year later, all 1,800 retail locations throughout the United States, the United Kingdom, Australia, and South Africa were simply called *Monarch*.

In 1999, Marc wondered what his customers would think of having Monarch Butterfly prepaid postage envelopes available upon card purchases. After testing Monarch Butterfly Postage in stores throughout New Jersey, Ohio, California, and Arizona, the results were a resounding YES! Most loyal customers preferred to have the option of selecting a pretty 'butterfly postage stamp imprint' matching envelope right there at purchase. By January 2001, all retail locations globally provided this service.

The next year, Marc's corporate jet went down.

*   *   *

Out of the blue over drinks at his place one day shortly after we met, he shared what happened.

"I'm on a return flight to Wisconsin when my captain came over the speaker to announce I should put my seat belt on. The second I clicked it … we literally fell out of the sky. Wind shear. Pointed straight for the ground. The last thing I remembered was the nose pulling up and as the plane leveled off, we crashed.

"I woke up in the hospital two days later out of a coma, with …" Marc took his hand from his neck and waved it down the scar to his knee. "… ninety-nine staples. Filleted like a fish I was.

"The medical team were amazed not one bone was broken."

Listening to his story, all I could do was shake my head with stunned awe.

"I was the only one who survived," was his conclusion.

I wanted to ask him how he emotionally resolved the traumatic experience. But as he bridged to make an obsessive fuss how our cocktails were far too low, and it was time for him to powder his nose … I had my answer.

*   *   *

Another brainchild of Marc's – the Monarch Television Network on cable – was launched in 2007 as a family entertainment vehicle featuring made-for-TV movies and situation comedies. The network developed its niche by remaking old movies of the week which originally aired in the 1970s and 80s by the three American broadcast networks: ABC, CBS, and NBC. By 2008, Monarch TV was available in over 70 million pay television households in the United States.

Initially, the unique cleverness of the movie remakes and sitcoms were well received by viewers simply wanting something different to watch. However, unable to deliver new movies and new shows timely meant far too many repeats. And viewership growth slowed, then reversed direction.

As Winston Clarke & Associates officially came on board in July 2009, the greeting card business was stalling out from the Great Recession. The doom and gloom of the economy and overall mental health of the country was going in the tank. No one felt like sending happy hi-de-ho greeting cards *just because* – let alone spend $4.95 on something they really didn't need to – unless, that is, someone died.

When the overall ratings of Monarch TV began to seriously plunge in 2008 to a free fall in 2009, Winston Clarke & Associates was handed the opportunity to fix everything in five minutes. And GO!

The first delivery was a new fall campaign entitled *Come Fly with Us*. For Monarch TV, the butterfly promo jingle and :30

second commercial spots complimented a strategic move to add nature-oriented television shows, documentaries and a Saturday morning lineup featuring four hours of children's programming in its October fall season launch. Television commercials were quickly produced for the greeting card division and aired on nearly all the cable and broadcast networks for the upcoming holidays.

2009 year-end growth in both divisions was so impressive, *Come Fly with Us* became the signature branding for all Monarch marketing in 2010. By 2011, the greeting card and products division was up 41% and Monarch TV viewership up by 37%.

And then came Marc's final idea, and quite possibly his professional undoing - Love Nōts. The concept was a disaster with legal. At this initial meeting, as the new agency of record for the new product, I ran my horse and pony show exhibiting the product and marketing campaign to the in-house attorneys. One of the Monarch Global lawyers stated that if this project went forward, he would bet his career he would be in court fending off lawsuits by 2020, if not sooner. Marc laughed and was quick to point out this meeting wasn't about the attorney's career or where he would be in a decade.

"This is happening. Everyone here today is to advise the best legal course to make this happen. So, advise," the President and CEO declared.

The room included six corporate lawyers who stared at one another, and immediately we were showered with advice.

"Make this a separate company – not under the Monarch umbrella."

"A Delaware LLC."

"These should not be placed in our stores. Walmart would be a better fit."

45

"Or online orders only."

"No advertisements on Monarch TV."

"Price them higher so children don't pass them around on Valentine's Day in class."

"$25."

"$30."

"$50."

"If someone hates someone that much to go out and buy one, they should not have a problem spending more money with all that rage."

"This sounds like someone going out to buy a gun."

"It's cheaper than a gun."

"It's a specialty card."

"It needs a warning label."

"Reverse psychology. Warn consumers: Do not buy, mail or give to someone you hate."

"That could have the opposite effect. Now it's a product for every individual who shouts, 'Don't tell me what to do!'"

"How many people are there who function this way?"

The room burst full of laughter.

"What about a positive element in the close – give the reader an option to improve themselves?"

And all eyes were upon their leader, Mr. Monarch.

"I'm glad to say you're all earning your pay for the day," Marc surmised, then said, "Okay. Yes, to everything. Except for the guns. Guns not included."

The room laughed again.

"Legal," Marc addressed, "set up Love Nōts as a Delaware LLC."

He looked at me. "Winston, work with legal on the product, packaging, and marketing. Use a warning label to its advantage.

Tell people what not to do so they will. Let's have some fun with this."

And within seven months, Love Nōts went live online and were indeed placed in the Monarch stores – as an outside vendor – in all their retail locations across the United States. They were marketed as comical little cards to never ever send or give to someone you don't love. Each card and envelope were wrapped in a clear plastic sleeve with a warning label. Six versions were launched as a test with a retail price of $100 and was received with overwhelming shock and awe … and buyers.

WARNING!

Do not purchase, mail, or personally deliver this to anyone. Violators who do, should not wear protective gloves from fingerprints while opening, handling, or mailing. Love Nōts will not be held liable for anyone following or not following this warning.

You really are one horrible person.
Your soul will take lifetimes to atone. Try loving yourself. And make amends with those you've hurt over and over again.
– *Unsigned.*
Because you're just an asshole.

We have completed the removal of daggers from our backs that are covered with your fingerprints.
Your soul has too many fractures to count. Try loving yourself. Put down the sword of a tongue inside that wicked mouth of yours. And say something nice to someone's face rather than shitting on their backside.
– *Unsigned.*
Because this a collective fuck you.

You are such an ugly human being.
The ache in your soul must be profound. Try loving yourself.
Look in the mirror and say – *I forgive myself for what I may
have done to myself and others.* And be nice. Nice is pretty.
– *Unsigned.*
   Because you're not worth it.

**The amount of energy you put into draining other's is
disgusting.**
Your soul must be completely exhausted. Try loving yourself.
And make right with those you have wronged.
– *Unsigned.*
   Because you don't deserve to know.

You are one rotten selfish human being.
Your soul has been consumed by the dark side. Try asking for
forgiveness from your victims.
– *Unsigned.*
   With Good Reason.

For years your likability has been less than zero.
Your soul is nearly dead. Try loving yourself. And get out of
the negative.
– *Unsigned.*
   Because this is my release of your toxic energy.

   As a national rage began to brew across the U.S. in 2010
following the Great Recession, the reverse psychology with the
Love Nōts marketing was brilliant – and an immediate hit. Ninety
percent of purchasers paid in cash versus using a credit or debit
card at retail locations. The $100 price was not an issue for

anonymous sweet revenge. And Love Nōts quickly became the highest profit margin product Monarch ever developed.

First year revenues crossed $80 million, and by the 2012 election cycle, sales more than doubled to $300 million. By 2014, sales passed the $600 million mark.

Love Nōts became so popular, running gags on TV had goaded The White House received more of these cards than any other piece of mail … with every elected official across the country as runner ups. "You're not a real politician until you receive a Love Nōt," one late-night host once joked.

The next year, two copycat companies jumped in this market with their own darker, nastier take on the anonymous moneymaker – *You Make Me Sick* cards and *Your Spouse Is Having an Affair* cards. Both enterprises took their messaging to the outer limits of mean and spiteful.

Once I had read every note these competitors produced, I strongly advised Marc to immediately pull Love Nōts from Monarch retailers. "They will damage our brand, and this will not end well," I pushed.

And then the unthinkable fell right into predicted play. On November 10, 2016, a suburban housewife in Scottsdale received her mail and within ten minutes stormed across the street to shoot her best friend in the face for 'sleeping with her husband'. Cynthia McDonald was charged with first degree murder and claimed *Your Spouse Is Having an Affair* cards pushed her over the edge.

By Christmas of the McDonald incident, two additional shootings by enraged recipients of *You Make Me Sick* and *Your Spouse Is Having an Affair* cards made headlines.

On December 26th, Marc himself declared enough was enough. Love Nōts were quietly pulled from every Monarch store, and he shut down the company and its online store lock, stock, and barrel.

There were no *I told you so's* by his legal team – other than prior planning was made for possible lawsuits that could flood in. Nor were there public apologies or mention of Love Nōts ever again. The lone company outside the Monarch shell simply vanished overnight.

And we all prayed the last of the killings were through – at least from anything relating to the genesis of Love Nōts.

Chapter Three

A Lazzara yacht over a hundred feet in length slowly voyaged by with a dozen partiers dancing on its back deck. Starboard in tandem, two WaveRunners cruised along at no wake speed through the Intercoastal on their way to the great Atlantic waters. We all waved our greetings. And I simply adored the now of where I was.

But my mind went back to Marc's levels of resignation on both personal and professional levels. Never married with no children, he lived his life doing anything and everything his way. His company evolved into what he wanted … with no one in the family to answer to as long as profits were to be made.

I've always known him as a man who gave 110% to growing the legacy he was given. A visionary with plenty of capital resources available whenever he so chose. So, this was one big step for Marc to choose surrender. One *astoundingly* big step, actually!

Brent came over to ask what I was drinking and if I would like another. "Vodka lemonade, please," I automatically replied, pulling myself out of deep thought. "No fruit," I added.

My cigarette had burned halfway down between my fingers. I ashed and puffed and saw Keith and Rafael strolling outside with two new guests behind them. They all walked over to the seating area by the manor entryway and made themselves comfortable.

As I debated whether it would be rude of me to stay put or be polite to stroll over to say hello, I smoked.

"Here you are Mr. Winston," Brent delivered.

"Please," I smiled, "Call me Win. Just Win."

"Like you *win*?" The cute kid jested.

Still smiling, I confirmed, "Exactly. Thank you for the refresher."

"My pleasure," Brent politely replied before returning to his station.

After one more drag to finish the smoke, I put it out, stood, grabbed my drink, and headed over to *The Keith and Rafael Show* for some laughs.

I stepped into shade provided by the high roof overhang to join the men seated around an enormous rough-cut chunk of white limestone serving as a cocktail table and fire pit, and immediately recognized Gary Bell, President of Programming with Monarch TV, as the man behind the reflective silver sunglasses.

"Hi, Gary," I happily smiled.

He stood and we hugged.

Mr. Bell was one of the first people I met when making the rounds of introductions as Winston Clarke & Associates was formally introduced to Marc's executive team as the new agency of record ... so many years ago. Gary had just started in the greeting card division as a junior copyrighter fresh out of college and was brought into our loop for the new ad branding sessions. His enthusiastic professional dedication and commitment to everything he did was beyond extraordinary – it was admirable. Of course, it was no surprise his trajectory up the Monarch Group ranks accelerated quickly to senior copyrighter, then to vice president of the greeting card division, then to a vice president in programming at Monarch TV, to where he was today.

And being the sporto exercise junkie he was, Gary would travel the world participating in triathlons for his vacations. One year, he climbed and reached the top of Mount Everest *for fun*!

Now in his mid-forties, he still could sexily be on the cover of any fitness magazine.

"May I introduce Lucas Romero," Mr. Bell said with pride. "We met at the London Triathlon last August, and have been running around together ever since."

A handsome young blonde twenty-something with sky blue eyes, Lucas stood in a white polo two sizes too small with a small Scooby Doo insignia stitched on the left breast, to deliver a nice-to-meet-you-hug with his ripped pecs and massive body building arms.

"I've heard a lot about you, Win," he said softly in an adoring British accent with a tender squeeze. Sitting down he added, "Gary is a big fan."

This was such a sweet and disappointing thing to hear. I knew there would be several people shocked and saddened to hear Winston Clarke was leaving his associates when the formal announcement was made on Monday. And Gary Bell would be at the front of this line.

"Thank you," I smiled. "Gary is a good one. You are very fortunate to have met this guy."

I took the empty seat on the other side of Gary, and he slapped my knee with a *So Good to See You* grin.

Tom and Jerry were seated on the left of Gary and Lucas; Keith and Rafael were to my right – with Rafael now puffing on his pot vape. Marc sat across the circle facing the manor to keep a watchful eye for new arrivals.

Keith kindly asked, "Lucas, what do you do?"

"Work out," was all he said.

Ten seconds of silence passed, and I quickly turned to Lucas and commented before one of these old buzzards could begin to peck, "When I was in the first grade, Lucas, my very first lunch box was covered with Scooby Doo and the gang."

Running my eyes across this group of a certain age – which was everyone but Lucas – I added, "Remember the metal boxes with the matching thermos inside?"

Lots of nods answered.

Marc sipped his drink with a grin – carefully watching my lead, knowing I was about to embark on something fun. I investigated his gaze and asked, "Did I ever share with you my Scooby Doo lunch box / babydoll nightgown nightmare experience?"

He laughed with intrigue. "I don't believe you have. And well, now you must."

"Then let me tell you all the story about the day I turned gay," I teased.

"And put on a babydoll nightgown for the first time?" Tom jested.

Keith launched into his day-long chuckle fest after every funny thing someone said – like the sidekick Ed McMahon had on *The Tonight Show* with Johnny Carson.

"And got caught masturbating watching Scooby Doo?" Jerry added.

I tittered and said with declaration, "If it were *only that enjoyable*. But oh, no. This. Was. *Worse*!

"First grade. Day one. I was number seven of eleven kids who jumped on board the bus in my neighborhood and got to pick out where we wanted to sit before anyone else. The seating selections were clearly defined by the 'older' kids – grades four and above – who claimed their rite of passage with the prime seats in the back of the bus. The last three rows were theirs. And never ever never sit there. *Or else!*

"So, I chose the center section of the bus. Right seat. Solo – behind my friend Louisa, who was my playmate since we were toddlers. I hopped on board, grabbed my spot and waved out the window to my mom. Well, I waved only once ... until it was pointed out how that was so uncool.

"'Don't be a pussy, Winston!' Skip Grush shouted. He was the older brother of my friend Daniel who was deaf. They lived three houses down.

"Daniel and I were in the same grade, but he went to a different school. So, this was the first time I was ever alone with his brother Skip. He could be a jerk to Daniel and me, but for the most part he left us alone.

"Unexpectedly, now I'm alone with Skip. In Skip's world. In a place that was rather scary and intimidating. His friends that were picked up for school in other neighborhoods were loud and bossy. And because they all sat in the back too, they'd all pass by me with some sort of glare – as if my greeting smile was inappropriate and bothersome.

"The bus ride was either heaven or hell – depending upon the time of day and everyone's sugar levels.

"Our driver Bob was an older fellow with a pack of Lucky Strike in his shirt pocket who just drove the bus. He never interfered with the socio-dynamics of what was happening to school or fro. So really, it was a free-for-all for the oldest kids to rule the roost as they so choose.

"Little did I know, I was instantly to become the bitch to pick on by Skip and his crew.

"I was always told I had the most beautiful blue eyes and was just an adorable towhead by everyone in my young universe – be it from family, my playmates' parents, or grownups from church. I had no idea I was a pretty boy.

"That is, until Kevin Handcock – and yes, that was his real name – one of Skip's loud-mouth friends I never met before had jumped on the bus and was immediately smitten.

"'Are you a boy or a girl?' He asked me on this first day of the bus ride.

"With a clean haircut parted on the side, wearing boys clothing, I found myself looking at Diana Kissel who lived down the street and rode horses – and wore boys clothing – wondering what kind of question was that? Diana was in the fourth grade, so she knew of and had experience with this kid.

"'He's a boy you dick!' Diana shouted to Kevin.

"'Well, you're the prettiest boy I've ever seen,' Kevin softly said before embarrassingly realizing his buddies just heard him. To realign his masculinity, the second grader turned to Skip and Co. squawking like a parrot, 'PRETTY BOY! PRETTY BOY!' generating the laughs he sought – at my expense.

"Five minutes! That's all it took leaving the safety of home on my first day of the first grade: flattered by a boy who thought I was pretty – yet feeling a sense of dread and unease about my entire future with these people.

"Louisa also had a look of shock that this older kid could be so rude. 'I think you're pretty,' she gently assured following this encounter.

"'Thank you. I think you're pretty, too,' I smiled in return.

"Jump to Day Three when a social nuclear bomb exploded before my eyes.

"I had boarded the bus and took my seat, when suddenly my mother burst from our home's open garage wearing a babydoll nightgown, racing barefoot, to deliver the Scooby Doo lunchbox I left on the kitchen table. And though she was well-endowed, I'd never seen my mother's breasts bounce and sway so violently in all directions as they did as she frantically came dashing our way. The sight looked gruesome and terribly painful.

"Bob reopened the bus door for her. All the kids rushed to the windows on the side for a better look. Abruptly, all eyes were watching Mom run.

"Our house had a longer-than-usual concrete driveway, and so her frantic rush took a while. A long while. And for me, the whole tit show was in slow motion, so it had plenty of time to forever sear itself into my brain.

"It was another experience I genuinely felt a strange sense that something was not right with my mother. And it was officially confirmed when she leaped upon the bus to personally deliver the lunch box into my little hands, completely unaware her left breast had fallen out from her babydoll nightgown – and was now greeting everyone with a raging *HI!*

"'Here you are honey,' Mother panted – so proud she was able to make this little moment right.

"I don't recall if I thanked her or not. I do remember, quite vividly, once she disembarked and walked back up the drive, I heard crickets, and all eyes were now on me – including Bob's from the long horizontal mirror above his head where he kept watch of the animals in his cage.

"The bus finally moved onward. And once everyone was back in their seats, Skip shouted, 'GOD DAMN WINSTON … YOUR MOM'S JUGS HAVE REALLY BIG NIPPLES!'"

* * *

The early bird guests laughed hysterically, howling.

"And Mama's teats were out!" Screamed Rafael.

"No wonder you're a big fairy, darling!" Marc teased.

"Sweetheart, I've been a cinder-fella since I was in Pampers," I volleyed back.

More laughs rolled.

Lucas asked with an air of confusion, "So which part turned you gay?"

"Actually Lucas, I've always been gay. Even as a little one. I didn't know what it was or what it meant. But I do remember when I was three, my father took me into the men's locker room and through the showers on our way to go swimming at the country club pool – and I was seriously aroused. I'd never seen so many cocks and balls. And man, from that day on I knew what I liked!"

The group gently laughed – completely understanding.

Still unclear, Lucas asked again, "But why did you say it was the day that *turned* you gay?"

Stepping in, Rafael injected condescendingly, "It was a lead to catch our attention … to jump into his story, Lucas."

"I was being facetious," I gently assured Gary's young man – still not reaching him.

As Lucas looked to Gary for clarity, I glanced around our group seeking for ideas on how this became so confusing.

Marc stepped in. "I can only imagine the course that day set into motion for you for the next twelve years of primary school, darling."

Keith spoke, "I want to know more about this cocky hand job kid. Was he always a bully?"

"He was," I nodded. "And Kevin was the only one. I never really experienced any bullying, except for him … and with an odd affection."

Changing the subject, Jerry asked if everyone has seen the array of beautiful cupcakes on the desert tower. "Marc, your spread of cupcakes has my mouth watering. What are all the flavors we have today?"

"Win had the cakes delivered this morning from Cream Yourself Bakery," Marc replied.

"I believe there are a dozen of everything," I added.

"Could that have been a red velvet whistling at me earlier?" Jerry laughed.

I nodded a taunting smile.

"Marc, I thought you had a 'bring-nothing' policy for your parties," Tom inserted with an edge of concern.

Without looking at him, Monarch replied, "You are correct Thomas."

Tom turned to Jerry with a *WTF* expression and the two looked back at Marc for further clarification. I glanced at Gary who dropped me a wink, rather amused by Tom and Jerry's sudden fret.

But our host abruptly caught sight of Antonio making his way through the house and stood to wave his high-priced call boy over.

Sporting a pair of black metal aviation sunglasses, out came this strappingly buff deeply tanned man's man with raven-black hair in a packed black Speedo. All eyes were on him. Actually, all eyes were all over him.

Marc motioned, "I'd like to introduce Antonio," he announced and ran the introductions.

Very politely, Antonio said hello to each of us then asked if we minded if he took a dip in the pool. Three 'Nos', two 'Not at all's, and one 'Please' were all said at once. He excused himself and Marc's hire walked over to the edge of the pool and looked into the crystal blue water with a long stare.

"Why does every gay party have an Agador?" Rafael quipped.

"His name is Antonio," Marc corrected.

"Does it *really matter* what his name is?" Tom spat.

The outdoor cast was quietly filled with anticipation of Antonio's next move.

"I hope he doesn't hurt himself thinking," Rafael sniped.

Reflecting on all the sexual servicing Antonio had provided him this past week, Marc commented with a proud smile, "Statuesque."

Antonio looked up and over at Marc with a beautiful smile then back into the pool.

A dozen seconds passed, and Keith finally declared, "I haven't experienced this much suspense since it was finally revealed who shot J.R.!"

A few of us laughed but no one took their eyes off the Brazilian god.

"I'm so sorry. Is J.R. a good friend of yours?" Lucas innocently asked Keith loud enough for everyone to hear.

I broke away from Antonio to see everyone look at one another in utter dismay as jaws dropped and pearls were clutched. All eyes rolled to Lucas.

Lucas caught everyone's disgust. "What?!" he softly shrieked.

Suddenly, there's a splash and Antonio was swimming – with his Speedo resting on the edge of the pool topped with sunglasses.

Rafael let out an angry murder scream and he stood in disbelief. Deliberately glancing at the pool, he wailed, "I MISSED THAT..." then turned to point at Lucas, "FOR THAT?!"

He gulped his glass dry and squawked, "Jesus God, it's time for shooters!"

As the large round man headed for the entry, he paused and turned to deliver a searing glare. "I could easily say something rather insulting and demeaning to someone in particular about now … but I *shan't*!"

Marc was not amused and visually followed Rafael's waddle – watching him disappear into the house. His lips pursed with disapproval, and he quietly went after him.

Tom declared, "You know every time that fat man speaks, all I hear is the sound of long fingernails scratching down a chalkboard."

Keith quipped to Lucas, "Don't worry about Rafael, he gets a little bitey when he doesn't eat something every ninety minutes."

"More like every ten minutes!" Jerry jabbed.

Tom pulled the damp bev nap from the bottom of his sweaty glass, and waved *WELCOME TO THE SHITSHOW!* like it was a flag, singing, "Ta-Da!"

Jerry stood and invited Tom for a refreshing view of the pool with a wink-wink.

As they stepped out of earshot, Lucas innocently commented, "Rafael reminds me of that guy in the movie *Beetlejuice*."

Keith shrieked, "Oh! For the sake of sweet baby Jesus and all of humanity, *NEVER EVER* say that in Rafael's presence. He *HATES* that comparison!"

Lucas sat stymied as though he had said a dozen wrong things at once.

Time for another smoke, I thought and stood and pulled my cigarettes and lighter from my pocket. Keith saw I was about to make my return to *Smoking*.

"Mind if I join?" he asked.

I smiled with a step out, then stopped and pivoted to Lucas.

"The first time I met Rafael, *Beetlejuice* was the first thing to pop in my mind, too." I said and gave the young man a wink and nodded a smile to Gary, who winked back in appreciation.

"Excuse me as I feed my beast," I tossed, popping a cigarette between my lips.

Keith and I made our way over and sat. Facing the pool, I toked. Keith was beside me in the direction the wind was blowing my puff. Catching this, I asked, "Would you like to switch seats, so the smoke doesn't go your way?"

"No. Smoke up, honey. I still love the smell," he smiled with enjoyment.

"Have you lost some weight?" I asked, quite serious, having noticed his jawline appeared a bit tighter since the last time I saw him. "You're looking pretty good."

He laughed. "Thank you," he said, "my back boobs are down three cup sizes."

I smiled and we sipped our drinks and Keith noted, "You haven't been to one of Marc's parties in a while."

Taking a drag and speaking smoke I replied, "Not since the time the police were called three different times and arrived three different times. When was that? About this time last year?"

"That was the Christmas party with Santa and his naked elves."

We looked at one another and cracked up.

"What was Marc thinking having six nude midgets at that gig?" I gaffed.

"Oh, that's why I must always attend," Keith declared. "There's always an atomic blast or two or five at Marc's parties and there's nothing better than a front row seat! His unscripted live reality shows are better than anything on his fucking TV network!"

We laughed again. Keith could be humorously witty – in the crudest sort of ways.

I smiled, commenting, "Rafael is in fine form today."

Keith moaned. "Oh … she's in one of her cunt moods. I wouldn't be surprised if she gets her ass thrown out within the hour, which will suck for her because I drove. And I have no plans of leaving until the party ends with *The Big Finish*. And she has a phobia of calling an Uber."

More laughs.

"Where's your electric plug-in thing with four wheels?" he taunted.

"I took a Lyft," I answered.

Watching Gary run his fingers through the side of Lucas's hair with adoration, I added, "Rafael doesn't care for the young ones, does he."

"He hates children!"

"I was referring to Lucas."

"So was I!" Keith shouted.

More laughter.

He continued, "Lucas is a young man boy. Legal. But a child, nonetheless. And I really feel sorry for him because that old fuck I've brought along has marked him as her chew toy for the day. I can tell."

I shook my head, rather amused. "For someone you dislike, you spend a great deal of time together."

Keith took a long sip of wine. "It's a like and loathe friendship, Win." He rolled onward, "Rafael is smart and funny, and overall decent person. And yes, he's an entertaining abortion I so adore watching behave badly. And we do feed off one another's banter. And he can royally piss me off! But it's our companionship that we both value.

63

"And what I find so funny is that he was Brien's friend long before Brien and I met. Honestly, I think Brien was Rafael's only friend in Florida. And during the fifteen years Brien and I were together, Rafael and I became sisters with one thing in common: Brien.

"And then we had the business.

"And when Brien died, we just kind of remained glued together as misfits who like to watch shit hitting the fan. And fortunately, when there is a lull or brief calm, Rafael is there to pick up a turd and toss it into a spinning blade."

Curious, I asked, "Could you ever see the two of you…"

Keith cut me off with a shriek and immediate look of disdain. "GOD NO! I find nothing physically appealing about that man. DO YOU?!" And with that, he shuttered with small gag.

We stared at one another's sunglasses for a few long seconds, then drank and returned to people watching. Tom and Jerry were still studying Antonio's swim as if they were at SeaWorld observing a dolphin perform back and forth swimming tricks in the pool. I looked to the house and saw a new group of arrivals mingling about inside.

"Why haven't you remarried?" Keith asked, kicking the topic to me.

I smiled and said with pause, "I … I threw myself into work when Chris died. He was the love of my life. And on that day … when it happened … my heart and soul collapsed."

*   *   *

My mind immediately went to that moment as though it happened an hour ago. It was January 2008, and I had just gotten home from work and walked into the kitchen talking on my new iPhone 1 with my sweet love, Union News Network correspondent Chris Copens, who was covering the war in Afghanistan.

"I have a surprise for you," he lovingly teased so far away.

I remember smiling. "You do?" knowing this was always his way of saying he was coming home soon.

"I'm flying out tomorrow at sunup and will be there in time to tuck you into bed," Chris whispered ever so sweetly.

I turned on the TV to the UNN 24/7 cable news channel.

"Hold on," he broke into his newscaster's voice. "I'm live again in ten."

UNN news anchor Andrea Smith was announcing Taliban insurgents had been launching a new round of bombings and we're going live to Chris Copans on the scene.

"Andrea, it's been another deadly day here in …" were his only words before a bomb landed right behind him. A bright orange burst of light shot around the world on live TV before the feed suddenly went black.

Returning to New York, the shocked news anchor immediately went to break.

All I could do is repeat his name into the phone – hoping he could hear my voice – as tears rolled down my face.

"Chris?

"Chris?

"Chris?

"Chris?

"Chris?"

*   *   *

Keith and I both drank. I smoked. And Keith was kind enough to allow a moment of silence to sit in for a bit.

"Well, you do have a reputation to uphold," Keith finally jested.

"I have a reputation?"

"You don't date. You don't put out. You're not a whore like the rest of we boys. You don't do the bathhouses or backrooms.

"And I tell you this only because I care. You have this off-limits aura."

"Well!" I gaffed, moving to lighten the mood. "I had no idea I was such a prude."

"You are honey!" Keith shout-laughed. "You've been a hot bachelor for years ... *and years*! And you really need to get back on the market."

"Says who?"

"Everyone!" Keith screamed as we shared a long stare at one another.

"You're the most eligible tasty kibble in town *everyone* wants to get a sample of. You are too good looking and too nice a guy to become an old maid."

"Well thank you for the five-cent therapy session, Lucy," I tossed.

"Maybe now is a good time to find your next prince charming. It very well may happen. Lightning can strike twice. And I hope it does for you, honestly."

I drank and smoked. "I believe in true love. And really, I don't have the desire to suck every cock in town. I've already done that."

"When did you suck every dick in town?"

"Back home, in high school. I did half the football team, most of the volleyball team, and several basketball players throughout my teens."

"You slut!" Keith screamed. "You never told me you were a Trixie Teen!"

I laughed. Then he laughed.

"Okay, so tell me about this Kevin hand job. Did anything ever come of this obvious crush he had on you since the first grade?"

I glanced at Gary and Lucas, catching them in a tender kiss from afar.

"Or is he straight?" Keith prodded.

"I don't know what he is today. Or was then."

In typical Keith form, he's got to hear the story – be it fact or embellished gossip.

"Well start from the beginning and don't leave out a single thing," he demanded. "Was he your *first*?"

I took a long drag of smoke. "No. My first was in fifth grade with Tony and Greg at a sleepover."

"Your first was a fifth-grade three-way? Oh my god!"

"Boys will be boys," I chuckled.

"Ok. Back to that in a minute. Get to the cock in hand! I want to know more about this Kevin!"

I relented to Keith on Kevin Hancock and began at the end. "My first week home from college for summer break after freshman year, Kevin stopped by my parent's house about ten-thirty on a weeknight and wanted to go party. He was dirty and stunk of sweat from cutting down trees all day. At nineteen, he had the hottest body and wore a pair of overalls with no shirt."

Keith chirped, "OH!"

"I had nothing to do but watch *Knots Landing* on TV, so I thought *why not*? He drove us around the country dirt roads in his work truck until he parked at this little spot under a covered bridge out in the middle of nowhere. Kevin had a bag of coke and I think we must have done … oh God … a dozen lines each."

"AND?!" He yelled.

"Kevin leaned over the bench seat to softly ask if he could watch me take a piss."

"The filthy pig!" Keith cooed.

I sipped my drink.

"AND?!" Keith shrieked. "That was your *in*! Did you let him?"

Watching Seth and Dell – who married over the summer at their home in Saugatuck – walk out to join Gary and Lucas, I confirmed, "Yes, it was. And no, I did not."

Keith released a moaning scream of disappointment. I looked at him realizing the more he and Rafael drank, they more they become sissy screamers.

"And why the fuck not?!" He demanded.

"After twelve years of his bully infatuations, the day had arrived for payback."

"You turned him down for payback?!" Keith bellowed, then roared with laughter. "Sweet revenge! I *LOVE* IT!"

I smiled as we stared at one another's sunglasses again as I took another long drag.

Still laughing, he yelled, "You were a tease! A horrible rotten little tease who wouldn't put out!"

"I would never put out for him!"

Drinking the last of my cocktail, I put out the smoke and rattled the ice cubes in my glass as a cue it was time to move on to another round of drinks. Keith gulped the last of his white zinfandel.

"And what did this Kevin do when you turned him down?"

"He took me home."

Wanting more, Keith asked, "And that was it?"

"Yep."

"Was that the only instance between you two?"

We're back at the sunglasses stare and as I smirked a silent pause, our outdoor bartender walked up.

"Refills?" Brent smiled.

Keith squealed, handing him an empty plastic wine glass, "Yes, please – chardonnay this time."

Brent picked up my glass. "Another of the same?" he asked. I nodded a smile.

Keith continued his infatuation with my history. "Oh! This is getting tasty! Now spill and tell the whole Kevin hand job story! What happened in high school?"

Teasing, I replied, "Maybe. Later. Maybe."

He laughed. "No, no, no! You're going to back up the train to elementary school right now and tell all from there!"

Pleased by and done with my smut story, I smiled then changed the subject. "Let's wait until there's an audience. We must share with the other children, Keith."

He hollered, "I could just scratch your eyes out right now!"

I cracked up over his theatrics. "You are hilarious! And might I suggest it's time you audition for another play? You've been off the stage for far too long, my dear."

"Oh, *that*!" he moaned.

"Yes, *that*! You need to get back on the horse."

I watched Keith pretend to ignore me as he watched a couple more people trickle out to the pool from the house.

Sadly, his last production was a disaster. Keith kept forgetting his lines and the show closed after two nights.

"You're very talented, Keith," I assured.

"Was," he said with melancholy. "I *was*."

We sat in silence for a moment, and I gently reiterated, "Think about getting back on the horse."

Keith turned to me with a frown and dropped a heavy sigh. "Win, there are times when I can't remember where I parked the horse. That's where I'm at, at this stage. On stage. Off stage. It can be an absolute blank. Where's the fucking horse parked?"

I reached over and clutched his forearm with an understanding nod. He patted my hand and nodded in return.

Brent returned and set the next round before us and cleaned the ashtray into a napkin.

"Thank you, Brent," we smiled.

Keith took a breath, reached for his wine, and licked his chops. "You know, I'm feeling peckish."

"There's food galore, go get something!"

"Can I bring you anything?" He stood and asked.

"Thank you, but I'll head in to grab a plate in a little while," I smiled. "I'll sit here … in the bad boys' spot."

Keith giggled and spontaneously froze with a look of alarm. "I think I have to shit," was all he said aloud before he quickly dashed to the mansion.

Watching him enter, I saw Tom and Jerry run inside following Gary and … just about everyone outside near the open wall. Something must have happened, but I didn't care.

This was a good moment for a time out, I decided, and reached for the phone in the left pocket of my shorts. There was one missed call from my sister since I arrived – which generally meant she was in a crisis and her hair was on fire. For a brief

70

second, I thought about turning the volume back on. But the phone went back in the pocket – now in Airplane Mode.

I returned to my drink and fired up another cig to continue chain-smoking. I saw Antonio step out of the pool dripping – perfectly nude. He sauntered over to a shaded table of nicely folded white pool towels and plucked one. Drying his ears, he caught sight of me then tossed the towel over his shoulder, grabbed another towel, picked up his Speedo, slapped on the sunglasses, and walked my way soaking wet naked.

He laid the dry fresh towel down on the seat cushion next to me with a beautiful smile. "Cheers."

I grinned. "Good swim?"

"Oh, yes," Antonio smiled.

"How many laps?" I asked.

"I don't know. I go until I'm finished. I never count."

Pointing to my cigarette case he requested, "May I?"

"Of course," I said.

He carefully pulled one out and put it between his beautiful lips. I leaned over with my lighter to fire it up. Following a long drag, Antonio thanked me. And we puffed.

Brent walked up for Antonio. "May I get you something to drink?"

"Please. A bottle of water," he answered then smiled at me. "I understand you are the winning ad man."

That was a funny way of putting it, I thought, cracking up.

"Winston. It's how I remember your name and what you do," he said.

"You are a master of word association."

"I have read all of Dale Carnegie's books."

Hot and intelligent ... no wonder Antonio was Marc's expensive favorite hooker.

"Marc shared with me how impressed he is by you, Winston. You've done well by him for a lot of years."

"Thank you, Antonio," I smiled, adding, "And Marc truly likes you."

"Yes. I am a convenient arrangement who does what he is asked," he grinned.

I laughed out loud and quickly decided not to share my thoughts on that. The vodka was kicking in and the restraint of my sexual tension was wearing thin. "May I ask you a professional question?"

Delivering a large smile with perfect white teeth, he replied, "Of course."

"I've never had a Q&A with a ..."

"Hired asset?" Antonio injected with a wink.

"Asset. Yes," I smiled.

"I enjoy talking about what I do," he touted, puffing on his cigarette. "What would you like to know?"

"Tell me about your life. How you went into this line of work."

Brent returned with a bottle of water. Antonio thanked him, cracked it open and guzzled.

Refreshed, he shared. While attending the University of Barcelona for his bachelor's degree in business, Antonio did some modeling to pay for the education. Upon graduation, he realized his dream of owning a gym. But the memberships didn't come in to keep up with the expenses. After he closed the business, he went where the immediate cash was – escorting.

"May I ask how old you are?"

"Of course," he politely smiled. "I'm thirty. I've been doing this for five years and have invested ninety percent of everything I've made."

"Good for you."

"I will retire in two years."

"That's fantastic! Where would you like to retire? Where would you like to call home?"

He laughed. "I've traveled all over the world and haven't decided."

"Have you thought about America?"

"No. I will visit. But I will not reside here." He looked up at the sky, around the Intercoastal and asked, "Have you traveled the world, Winston?"

"Not like I've wanted. I was busy working. But change is in the air. Greece is on my list."

"Greece is lovely," Antonio said with great fondness as he watched more guests flow out from the house. "Quite stunning. I could live *there*."

And with a suave smile, he turned to me with a beautiful look of wisdom. "After you have traveled all over the world, I would like to ask if you will stay in America."

I thought for a moment and confirmed, "I would like that."

"Marc tells me you have been a bachelor for some time. I'm sad to hear of your departed."

I pursed my lips together and said nothing for a moment. "Relationships take a tremendous commitment and require a great deal of attention. Love can be bliss until Life strips it away without warning. I haven't felt the need to reinvest yet."

Antonio watched me quietly, taking a couple drags off his cigarette ... then asked, "Do you have your phone?"

"I do."

He held out a gorgeous tanned hand with finely manicured long fingers.

I removed the iPhone from my shorts, unlocked it, and passed it.

Smiling, Antonio commented, "I just got a new iPhone from a client as a bonus. It's like this one."

He typed away, returned the phone, and added with a smile, "Now you have my contact. I like you. And if you would like some attention without the commitment, you know how to reach me."

"Thank you," I smiled … flattered I've just been solicited by a pricey international prostitute.

"Now I must freshen up to be available to Marc," he grinned.

"I understand," I said catching sight of Marc walking towards us carrying a drink in each hand. His saunter was slowing again, I noticed, and picked up my cocktail for a sip.

"Here you are, darling," Marc greeted, placing an overflowing cocktail on a coaster before me.

Holding the one I just received from Brent in hand, Marc snatched it away, and hurled the glass and drink into the Intercoastal, making a plunking splash. "Fresh is better!" he insisted.

I burst into laughter.

"I hope the two of you got to know one another," Marc added.

"As you said," Antonio politely gleamed, "Winston is very engaging."

"Of course, he is," Marc glowed. "How was your swim?"

"Quite nice. I was just about to go freshen up."

"Sounds fabulous," Marc chirped.

Antonio stood. I watched the outside partygoers stop and turn for a view of the naked God. He wrapped the towel around his waist and tossed the Speedo on his right shoulder before delivering us a big smile, and headed in.

Lowering my sunglasses to purposely lock eyes with Marc, I declared. "Worth every penny, darling."

"Cheers to thaaaat, daaaarling," Marc toasted with his glass in a long slur as he plopped himself in a seat beside me.

"Was a cliffhanger from *Gays of Our Lives* unfolding inside?"

Marc gasped with annoyance. "Two uninvited misfits were having a heated snit and decided to deck it out by the crab legs. One went down and the other jumped on top to punch and punch, and punch. It took a few brawn men to pull them apart and boot them out the door. Where is my security detail when I need them?"

"Oh my," I declared with a hint of caring, but didn't really.

He sighed deeply and said, "Before I jump into grilling, I have a little something to offer you."

I grinned and lifted my eyebrows.

"You remember my ex, Xavier?"

"Yes, from Manhattan. He was here at one of your parties last year."

"A few months back, I purchased a transatlantic cruise for the two of us next March in a presidential suite. And after we broke up – as friends – Xavier said he still would like to go. But he flew in a last month for a possible make-up visit and, well, that didn't go very smoothly. He has since bowed out of the trip.

"I was thinking, now that you are about to have time on your hands, how wonderful it would be for you to join me. It's already paid in full. A ten-day cruise from Fort Lauderdale to Barcelona. We could spend a week or two in Spain touring the country. And my jet will fly us home."

Speechless. That's what I was. Honestly, I didn't feel I could spend that much time with him – ten days trapped on a ship with two weeks countryside. No thank you!

"The suite is two floors with a bathroom on each floor. The sofa in the living room pulls out to a lovely bed."

I still had nothing to say but did hear my mind scream *There is no way in hell I would ever sleep on a sofa bed across the Atlantic!*

"Unless you want to sleep with this fat fuck who snores like a banshee."

I was filled with gratitude for the thought. But no. This was never going to happen.

"I'm actually seeing myself on the other side of the world clicking out my novel on a laptop."

"It's an idea, darling!" Marc shrieked as if that were a *Yes!* He held up his drink for another toast.

"Thank you, though." I smiled forcefully for the oncoming cocktail tap. "It truly is a generous idea."

"You're turning me down, aren't you?"

"I am declining the invitation," I said as my smiled relaxed.

"Then you must share a family funny," Marc relented. "When was the first time you realized something was wrong with Mother?"

"The first shocker was when I was four. I was watching a cartoon or kids show and a commercial came on with this fantastic toy. What it was I don't recall. But I went gaga spastic over it and Mom *had* to see this commercial.

"Well, Mother was asleep in bed … as she was most every day until noon or so. And this was early in the morning, possibly just after Dad went to work or go play golf.

"So, I ran down the long hallway of the bedroom wing as fast as my little legs could go, screaming, 'Mom! Come here quick! Mom! Mom! Come here! Mom!'

76

"I opened her bedroom door with a hyper yelp, 'Mom! Come quick!' then I raced back to the TV in my bedroom.

"She came rushing in her customary babydoll nightgown, completely disoriented, still half asleep, scanning all around to see what was happening.

"'Look!' I shouted and pointed to the TV as the very last second of the commercial played off. 'That's what I want for Christmas from Santa!'

"Thinking the house was on fire or something detrimental was taking place, she shook her head then clutched her heart. 'This was about a television commercial?' she gasped in disbelief.

"I was jumping up and down nearly out of my mind with excitement, when Mother impulsively shrieked, 'This was about a toy? OH WINSTON ... THIS WAS ABOUT A TOY COMMERCIAL?!'

"And with that, she collapsed onto the 70s green shag carpeting and whimpered like she just received a jolt of electroshock therapy."

Marc had both sets of fingertips draped across his mouth as if that would contain the choke-giggles. His eyes began to water as he exhaled with exasperation.

"That was Mother's first one?"

"That I recall."

He took a long deep breath like a mental orgasm exploded satisfactorily and thanked me.

"I should go in and have an appetizer to neutralize some of the booze," I said with a strange sense my mother-stories were tweaking Marc in some peculiar fashion.

"Yes, and I should get things ready to set the meat on fire."

I extinguished my cigarette and stood. "Think I'll begin with some of your beautiful caviar."

"Please do! None of the anorexics here will ever pick up a plate."

Placing his hand on my forearm he added, "And love, if you feel as if you would like a quicker picker upper …" then snorted an imaginary sniff, "simply help yourself. I'm due for a touch up here again shortly."

I wasn't going to remind him he already made the offer earlier. Rather, I placated, "Marc, you know I'm a Nancy Reagan."

"Oh, Nancy," he slurred like a whining adolescent, "Yes, yes, yes! Say no to drugs … say yes to booze … drugs are bad … liquor is better."

Then Marc shifted to a sarcastic agitated tone and said, "*Liquor*?! God no! *YOU* lick her!"

I laughed, watching him scoot off the edge of the chair for momentum to stand – rather pleased with his humorous point.

"If you do get the itch darling, everything is in the storage island in my dressing room off the bath. The code for entry is 925," he taunted. "Think of Jane, Lily, and Dolly in *9 to 5*. It's the only way I can remember any of the codes around this place," he said as he took my arm in his and we walked to the manor.

Terrific. *9 to 5* was now tuning in my head and I'm dangerously thinking how a tasty reunion with the ex-refreshment I swore off twenty years ago would be.

Thanks Nancy!

Chapter Four

Returning indoors, dozens of new arrivals were milling about – many of whom I'd seen at various events and galas throughout town. We smiled hellos, and I found myself merging behind Tom and Jerry who were also in route to the appetizer buffet. Rafael stood midway at the blue granite counter in the kitchen, chomping on a prawn lathered in cocktail sauce as the three of us made our way past him to a stack of white China plates.

Following Tom and Jerry, Tom said to Jerry loud enough for Rafael and me to hear, "Let's plate up and eat on the patio *with the civilized.* Watching *that one* chomp and slurp reminds me of feeding time at the Miami Zoo."

"Yes, yes," Jerry auto-replied, more focused on the tower of cupcakes than a snark from his husband.

Jerry turned to me with fret. "Dare I begin with dessert, or wait until after the BBQ?"

With a cocky grin, I pursed my lips and said, "You got me, Jerry. That's a tuffy!"

Grabbing control of himself, moving on to the seafood, Jerry sang whimsically, "*Good things come to those who wait.*"

Tom and Jerry quickly progressed along the line of food barely dressing their plates with a single of this, another of that, a lone raw baby-cut carrot, and celery stick. By the time they zoomed off, I managed to spoon Ossetra caviar onto several water crackers and was going for the shrimp.

"You missed the Gladiator fights," Rafael announced as he began to shadow me.

"I gather."

"It was very butch until they began kicking and screaming over the eviction."

"Did you catch what the tussle was all about?" I asked, reaching for tongs to pick up a few pieces of seafood nicely spread across beds of crushed ice.

Rafael paused his next bite, holding a prawn in the air. "I think one of them was Mr. Leatherman of the Year. Ages ago. And his little buddy was a sassy man chewing on his ass about fucking his roommate … or something along those lines.

"Having enough, Mr. Leatherman turned around right there center stage and shouted, 'So what if we sucked and fucked?! Just who in the fuck do you think you are?!'

"Then little one threw the first punch. Leatherman grabbed him by the neck. And down they went into a wrestling match. It was all very machismo."

I decided I had plenty of starters and turned to see if the club chair I sat in earlier with Marc was available. It wasn't.

With a strange excitement about it all Rafael continued, "I must confess, I was rather impressed with Gary's Scooby Doo … because when they ran in, Scooby dove right into the WWF kerfuffle without a second thought and pried little one off Leatherman lickety-split. Several of the other guys then stepped in with Gary to pull Leatherman off the floor and physically showed the two the door."

I stood for a moment watching him gnash into the prawn with his big teeth – and never realized how fucking large Rafael's teeth actually were. Right then, he looked eerily dangerous.

Recalling I had set my cocktail down by the stack of plates, I declared aloud, "My drink," as a breakaway from Rafael's face to the starting line where I first began. With cocktail back in one hand and food in the other, I looked for a place to park as Rafael bookended me. Ignoring him, I caught a clear space at the other end of the kitchen island and coyly said with discovery to myself, "Ah! There's a spot," and headed that way.

Resting my glass on the edge of the blue granite, I turned to see Rafael had been hot on my heels. Resigned to the reality my body needed nourishment that wasn't from a glass … I really cared less where the fat man stood and picked up a topped cracker to inhale and watched Robert Palmer's 80s music video *Addicted to Love* on the TV wall. I bit into a second round of caviar when Ron Saltz and Steven Wolfe approached with smiles and beverages in hand.

"Win!" smiled my real estate agent, Ron. "My God, it's been forever! How the hell are you?" he teased, since we just saw one another Wednesday at the closing of the WC&A Building … before he landed an awkward bear hug upon me as I munched a tight-lipped grin.

Steven winked at me then cocked his head in disapproval over Ron, rolling his eyes that one just doesn't squeeze a person in the middle of a chew.

Ron pulled away and I called him a big goof.

Suddenly, a loud commotion from the foyer caught our attention with the arrival of Stephan Denino and his longtime personal *whatever*, Edward.

"And what do we have here?" Rafael curiously prompted before walking that way for a closer inspection.

"Oh, terrific … it's The Steph and Ed Show," Ron dropped with sarcasm to me and Steven, adding before he darted to the patio, "Think I'll go see if the skinny dippers are out yet."

I saw Marc enter from the deck and cross paths with Ron, who paused to give him a hug. As the two stood a moment to chat, Steven Wolfe, the president of Las Olas Bank, leaned into me, gently grasped my right arm, and whispered into my ear, "A little birdie told me your building sold."

Pulling back with a delighted smile, Steven so very softly added, "We funded the buyer. Congratulations." He then pretend-zipped his lips sealed.

I winked back with a muted, "Thank you."

Out of the blue, we heard someone break into a roaring sob in the Stephan Denino region. Everyone indoors paused. The house went silent. All our eyes were now on this new show, as Marc made his way to whatever was happening.

From my vantage, I could see Stephan shake his head … Marc stepped into console … and Edward blurted out something was *really horrible*.

"What happened?!" We all heard Marc plead loudly.

"Someone kidnapped Stephan's Barbie doll collection Thursday morning!" Edward shouted.

"THEY DID MORE THAN THAT, EDWARD!" Stephan shrieked.

Standing close to the action, Rafael turned to look at me and Steven with a twisted grin of amusement. I looked back at Stephan who collapsed into drunk Marc's open arms for a hug … nearly taking them both down before Edward caught the two and scooted them over to a couple open seats at the bar to prop them up. I looked at Rafael, who was still wearing an unsavory grin.

"Think I'll join Ron," Steven said breaking away. I should have followed his lead but was strangely magnetized to whatever this was and slowly walked over to the train wreck.

Marc turned to Brad the bartender with a heated sense of *DIAL 911!* urgency. "Quick! Two rum and Cokes!"

"Diet!" Stephan and Edward modified the order in unison.

"Start from the very beginning, darling," Marc said calmly, taking Stephan's trembling hands into his.

"Well, I need everyone to put on their Perry Mason caps and give me all you've got since the police don't consider this a high priority," Stephan opened, wiping a tear of distress from his cheek.

I looked around the room to see all eyes were latched onto Stephan's next syllable. It was a strange sight – with nearly every guest wearing the same facial expression Carol Burnett would have in that lightning second before she would have to look away from Tim Conway or Harvey Korman to keep from breaking character in a skit and fight off a fit of laughter.

Stephan continued. "Well, at 7 am Thursday on my way out the door, I said goodbye to the girls, set the alarm, and went to the office to meet the delivery truck from the printer and five drivers who distribute the magazine – without a clue that evil was about to set its clutches upon my beautiful babies."

Their cocktails were delivered, and Marc swiftly passed them to Stephan and Edward, who gulped them dry. Marc immediately requested another round from Brad.

Wiping more tears of fret away, Stephan took in a long breath after chugging his drink and resumed. "Nothing seemed out of the ordinary. The pallets were dropped off, the drivers loaded their vans, I cleaned up the pallet wrap film and decided to go home for an early lunch. The very minute I pulled into the garage and saw the alarm to the house was turned off I knew something was amiss."

Rounds of questions fired from the crowd:

What time was this exactly?
How often do you change the code to the alarm system?

Who else knew the alarm code to your house?
Don't you have security cameras on the property?
What were you wearing?

Marc glanced at me with astonished annoyance.

Stephan answered in order. "Eleven fifteen. I've never changed the code. My housekeeper. I don't have security cameras. Navy shorts with a fun yellow Gap shirt, Birkenstock clogs and my jewels." He held up his hands to proudly display the variety of diamond rings he wore on seven fingers.

"You walked into the house and *then* what happened?!" Marc demanded, getting the story moving again as I stepped in beside him.

"It's all a fog … I mean, I entered the kitchen, threw my keys on the counter and out of the corner of my eye, I saw a flicker of light and my stomach fell out. You know, the kind of sinking feeling you get when you know something is terribly *terribly* wrong – like when Sigorny Weaver slowly turned around to see the alien breathing on her?

"Well … I ever so carefully turned my head to see the wall of glass hutch built-ins completely emptied with one of its doors half open. The whole room screamed *Violation!*"

As several gasps rolled from the crowd of listeners, Brad handed Marc the refills and he passed them to Stephan and Edward, and desperately asked, "My God, Stephan, what did you do then?"

"I clutched my chest and slowly walked into the living room, not even thinking the intruder could still be in the house. I carefully stepped over to the open hutch door and saw a Polaroid lying in the center case where my first issue of Barbie once proudly stood in her box."

Stephan pulled a sheet of paper from his murse and held it out for all to see. "This!" he sighed with exasperation, passing Marc's way.

"It's a color photocopy," Stephan clarified.

Marc took a strong look. He turned to see I was now beside him and handed me the evidence with eyebrows raised.

The copied Polaroid was a blindfolded vintage Barbie with the black curly updo, stripped naked with its hands and legs tied together with a red piece of yarn, and a revolver pointed to its head. Written in black marker across the bottom white tab read:

CALL COPS, SHE TAKES A BULLET!
WILL BE IN CONTACT.

"Did you call the police?" someone asked as the photocopy was passed around the bar.

"Of course!" Stephan shrieked.

"What did they say?" another guest in the crowd yelled.

"Before or after they broke into laughter?" Stephan fired back.

As tisks and disapproving sighs bowled about, Marc patted Stephan's arm and calmly said, "How typical."

"It was intuitive," Stephan added. "You get robbed; you call the police."

Marc nodded to keep the story moving.

"I had to have a police report to file an insurance claim," Stephan added looking into Marc's eyes.

Most of us quickly glanced at one another. I saw new arrivals had expanded the crowd of listeners and noticed Rafael had moved right behind me.

Marc then cocked his head that read, *Okay, let's get this thing moving ... I've got a party to tend to!*

Stephan resumed, "Well, then, I quickly made a copy of the Polaroid in my home office since I knew it would be taken into evidence and would undoubtedly need something for my insurance agent."

All eyes are back on him.

"What else was I to do?" Stephan went on the defense. "My girls are worth a million and a half dollars! And millions more sentimentally!"

He paused to read the room.

"Anyway, the police should be able to find the Eddie's Electrics delivery truck with two-thousand one-hundred and seventy-three collectible Barbie dolls all huddled together!"

"How do you know it was an Eddie's Electrics truck?" Rafael inquired.

"Because Mr. Swartz across the street reported he saw an Eddie's Electrics truck back into my driveway around 8 a.m. He thought it was making an early delivery ... when in fact, it was the kidnappers plucking my babies from the safety of their home and loading them into a cold truck."

The photocopy made its way back to Stephan. He gently caressed it and sadly added, "Oh, how could anyone in their right mind strip, tie up, blindfold and shoot such a beautifully innocent baby girl?"

"When was Barbie shot?!" Marc yelled.

"I DON'T KNOW!" Stephan yelped, then choked. "There was no way I could stay in the house with the alarm system compromised ... so Edward and I stayed at the Hilton on the beach Thursday night and last night and found this under the wiper blade of my car this morning on our way here!"

He pulled an actual Polaroid from his murse and held it high in the air to show his audience. "It's a picture of my precious baby ... *MURDERED*!"

The room gasped.

A handgun was beside Barbie's naked body. And written on the white tab in red marker read:

YOU CALLED COPS!
MORE TO DIE!
I SAID TELL NO ONE!

Stephan handed the Polaroid to Marc.

Still holding my plate of remaining appetizers, I popped a shrimp into my mouth as Marc held the photo out for me to grab. I placed my plate on the bar and closely looked at the graphic setup staged for the picture, then turned and gave it Rafael.

"Yep," Rafael declared matter-of-factly. "Her plastic head was blown clean off – nothing but the stub of her neck."

The room gasped again then moaned with disapproval. Though it did sound as if someone broke into laughter somewhere in the mix of onlookers – and quickly shut it down.

"What?" Rafael shrugged with surprise the room instantly turned on him. "She's dead!" he declared and passed the photo along to another guest.

Stephan burst into a roaring sob. Marc took him into to his arms and glared at Rafael. The show was over, and guests began to meander outdoors.

I turned and nudged Rafael with a look *it's time to walk away.* Leading I asked, "Who could have done such a thing?"

Keith was headed in our direction from the half bath off the kitchen.

With a wicked smirk, Rafael affirmed, "Who knows? That man has a hundred enemies," and with a shift in tone that sounded rather excited, he added, "But it does appear a murder mystery is afoot."

"What happened?!" Keith shrieked. "What did I miss?!"

Rafael replied with an odd pleasure in his voice, "*Step-Han's* Barbie collection was stolen, and one was killed because he called the cops. Apparently, Victim Barbie was stripped completely naked, tied up with yarn and her head was shot clean off."

"Oh my, God!" Keith blurted aloud. And with this mental image now burning inside him, he spontaneously combusted with laughter. "*Oh my, God!*" he screamed again, covering his mouth with a hand, yowling.

Oh, Fuck! my mind shrieked in panic. This was highly inappropriate.

Shifting my position so my back was to Marc and Stephan, I insisted to Rafael under my breath, "Move this screaming Mimi outside *ASAP*."

We both looked at Keith, who was laughing louder by the second. "*OH MY, GOD!*" he laugh-screamed another notch in volume.

"*Exactly how*, Winston?!" Rafael snapped back with a frantic look Keith had become an unstoppable fiasco.

"I'm smoking," I said with swift resignation, and bolted like Bambi catching sight of Elmer Fudd on opening day of Deer Season.

Chapter Five

As I stepped through clusters of giggling and gossiping guests, I heard the words *Barbie* and *Stephan* pop from all directions while fumbling to get a cigarette fired up. At *Smoking*, I discover all the seats were taken by young men I didn't know who weren't smoking. It's then I realized I left my drink on the kitchen counter and was empty handed.

My gaze moved to the tiki bar where I saw a group of four walk away with fresh cocktails, opening a space for a clear shot to Brent. With a long drag of smoke, I decided it was time for a change in drink and stepped up to the bar for a seat. On my right were two adorable young blonde tan buff buddies in their twenties I hadn't met, who were talking about how they used to play with Barbies when they were boys.

Brent handed them fruity cocktails and looked at me with his beautiful smile.

"It's about time I dial it down a bit," I sighed, slightly exasperated. "Do you have Pinot Grigio?"

He did and reached for a bottle from one of the small refrigerators behind him.

The striking young man on my right tossed out an "Oooh! That sounds like a fun drink! What's in it?"

I paused, thinking this is exactly what I needed – a genuine excuse to laugh. And I did.

"Grapes," I said with a teasing smile.

"Like grape juice?"

I laughed a bit more. "Exactly!"

Brent placed a filled glass before me, having caught my having some fun with the young men his age.

"It's a white wine. Not sweet but not too dry," he politely informed those who didn't know.

Another "Oooh!" was cooed before the young man introduced himself as Michael and leaned back to reveal his equally cute partner. "And this is Steven."

Raising my glass for a toast, I said, "I'm Win. Nice to meet you Michael and Steven. Cheers!"

The young ones didn't pick up their glasses or tap or drink for *Cheers!* They simply said the word as if it were a YAY emoji.

A thought of mentoring these kids on proper *Cheers!* etiquette crossed my mind but moved to their conversation on playing with Barbies.

I injected, "I used to play with my neighborhood girlfriends' Barbies when I was a tot."

"I had my own," Steven announced.

"I had to play with my sister's," Michael added. "My parents wouldn't let me have Barbie or Ken."

"I don't know if they still make them, but Santa brought me a Big Jim doll one Christmas. He was a taller clean-shaven version of G.I. Joe, and I spent hours playing with it," I said.

"I had G.I. Joes," Michael proudly added. "And I'd take all their clothes off when I'd go to bed at night, and they'd sleep with me."

This was now going down a road I thought best less traveled, and asked, "How do you know Marc?"

"Marc, who?" Steven leaned across Michael and asked.

"The host of today's party," Brent answered, shifting his eyes to mine with a curious look.

Michael jumped in, "Oh! We know Marc from The Banana Peel. Steven and I are strippers there."

"Clothing optional performers," Steven clarified with a smile prominently revealing he was missing a mid-molar tooth from the upper left side of his mouth.

"That's a lovely gaping hole in your face," I wanted to point out, but opted to go with, "I have to say … I have never been to The Banana Peel."

"You should!" Michael pitched.

"Stop in!" Steven added. "We perform Sundays through Thursdays, two to ten."

Michael nodded with pride.

"I'll have to put that on my Bucket List," I smiled, trying to sound like this was an opportunity of a lifetime.

"It was so nice to meet you, Win, but we are starving and haven't eaten since last night," Michael declared.

"There is so much to feast on," I said motioning to the house. "Please, go eat."

"Nice to meet you, Win," Steven smiled with that hole.

"Yes. We'll see you around," Michael added before the two scooted off.

As I took a drag, Brent set a clean ashtray before me.

"Thank you, Brent," I smiled, ashing the cigarette. I turned for a look to see if *Smoking* cleared. It hadn't.

Then I caught Bill and Gill walking my way, each holding a glass of white wine, wearing smirks that shouted *I'm Over This Already*.

The rhyming duo owned Hints of Tints – the renowned art gallery wealthy connoisseurs from all over the world frequented when visiting South Florida. With their anchor gallery on Las Olas Boulevard open year-round, Bill and Gill also had a sister boutique gallery in Provincetown they ran during the summer season. I'd known the two since I moved to Fort Lauderdale decades ago and always enjoyed chuckles over their primness.

I hopped off the bar stool for hugs. Bill stepped in first, followed by Gill. And they sat in the two seats left by Michael and Steven.

"Enjoying the show?" Bill asked with a hint of sarcasm.

"I'm beginning to feel saturated from all the Steve's, Steven's, and Stephen's here," I replied.

"Honey, I've been choking on those names since I moved to town in the 90s," Gill gaffed.

Bill joked, "Every Stevie south of Palm Beach needs their own dog tag identifiers – Banker Steve #71, Bartender Steve #38, Real Estate Agent Steve #465, Mechanic Steve #22, Professor Steve, Parking Meter Maid Steve, Drunk Steve, Barbie Steve ..."

Gill and I are giggling.

"I just met Stripper Steve," I added.

Gill roared.

Pleased with his point, Bill smiled and stopped for a sip of his wine, then said, "It would appear a crime has been committed in someone's mind."

Gill broke from his happy place and shouted, "Oh my God!" and continued with all seriousness, "The way Stephan has incessantly jabbered about how valuable that infamous Barbie doll collection of his is – *forever* to anyone who gave two farts to listen – I'm not surprised something like this hasn't already happened."

I decided to bridge on to something else and complimented how well each looked and asked how their summer was in P-Town. Gill proudly flaunted the 'little work' each of them had done around the eyes and neck. Bill quickly shifted topics again and announced their gallery in Provincetown had its most lucrative year ever.

"A crypto billionaire stopped in and bought eighty percent of the store right on the spot," he announced. "For a mansion he was building in South Carolina with thousands of feet of walls to cover."

"That was over Memorial Day Weekend!" Gill exclaimed, beginning the tag team response he and Bill always ran. "Can you imagine, launching the summer season with an empty gallery?"

"Fortunately, we had plenty of pieces in storage leftover from the Covid-19 years to replenish the inventory."

"And if wasn't the grace of God, I don't know what it would be called ... but a trust fund baby like Marc stopped in the week before July 4th and she bought nearly everything on site for a McMansion she and her wife have in the Adirondacks."

"Marc inherited the family business, he's not a trust fund baby," Bill corrected.

"Well, she inherited her family's trucking business and is a gazillionaire whatever she does. It doesn't matter."

"We literally flew back here July 10th, packed up the entire collection from the Las Olas gallery, and drove it up to Provincetown in five days – just so we had product for the rest of the season."

"By Labor Day, ninety percent was sold."

"Unheard of!"

"Will never happen again."

"The gallery looked as though we were going out of business."

"We were literally down to the bare walls with a little of this on a shelf here, a thing or two over there."

In unison they closed with, "Amazing!"

"That's incredible!" I congratulated. "Now that you're back for the winter what are your plans?"

Bill and Gill quietly looked at one another with mischievous grins.

Bill spoke as Gill sipped his wine, "We're done, Winston. We've run these two galleries for nearly twenty years and, we're just ... toast-a-roonies."

Gill leaned across Bill to softly say, "We're putting both galleries on the market."

"The buildings," Bill corrected, again.

"Yes," Gill agreed and leaned back into his bar stool as Bill nodded with an *It's True!* relieved grin.

Astonished the three of us were literally on the same page, I itched to share my news ... but couldn't. I would be in breach of contract if I said anything before the formal WC&A announcement was made on Monday. Knowing I was already in breach by sharing the details with Marc, I bit my tongue instead and raised my glass for a *Cheers!* And we tinked with drink.

I took a drag from my cigarette and they tisked in disapproval.

"You're not in *Smoking*," Gill reprimanded with a teasing tone – referring how Marc would say that to anyone who fired up outside the designated area.

"*Smoking* is filled," I said and looked over as confirmation.

"Cigarettes are not good for you, Win," Bill said.

"Yes, they are," I smiled.

"No, they aren't," Gill added.

Unmoved, still smiling, I confirmed, "Yes, they *are*."

"You should quit," Bill said.

"No, I shouldn't," I replied.

Both rolled their eyes and shook their heads in disagreement.

"When did you begin that nasty habit?" Gill asked.

"When I was twelve or thirteen."

"Why would you start smoking at that age?" Bill asked.

I thought back and said with a chuckle of awareness, "Goodbye to Sandra Dee."

"What?" They asked together.

"My mother took me to see the movie *Grease* when it came out in what, 1977. I would have been twelve.

"It was at the end, when Sandy decided to make a change for Danny," I smiled with recall.

"I was having an identity issue like Sandy and didn't want to be the goodie two-shoes anymore either. And when Olivia Newton John stood out in her tight black leather jacket and pants, in those fantastic pumps ... smoking a cigarette ... I wanted to be her. I wanted to be cool. So, I bought a pack of Salem Lights and joined the naughty kids in the neighborhood. And said goodbye to Sandra Dee."

Bill and Gill sat staring into my eyes with a dismayed sadness, covering their mouths with their hands, speechless.

Another sip of wine and another drag of smoke, and I was ready to move on and asked what they were going to do next.

Bill and Gill lit up with tremendous enthusiasm.

"A whole lot of nothing!" Bill joyously sprang.

"Amen to that!" Gill gleamed.

"Amen to *that*!" I echoed in unison.

And in that moment of jubilance, I recalled Stephan Denino's office for *Outrageous Magazine* was next door to their art gallery. In fact, Stephan was their tenant.

"Does Stephan know you're selling the building?" I inquired.

"Yes," they said together.

Bill clarified, "We disclosed the intent to him two weeks ago."

We stared at one another for a long moment – my eyes bouncing between Bill's and Gill's.

"He asked if he could make the first purchase offer," Gill said.

"We reluctantly said yes. But in all reality, we don't know if he can do it. He has until next Wednesday to submit a formal offer or it's officially on the market."

"*Well*," Gill tossed with suspicion, "if he collects the insurance for those fucking Barbies, he could do it."

I didn't mention Stephan was wealthier than anyone knew.

"Did you catch in there, how there wasn't a ransom note? Doesn't a kidnapper generally want a ransom? I take – you give – then you get back what I took." Gill clearly outlined. "The *Don't Call Cops* scribble is nonsense. It means nothing. Something is amiss with this whole storyline."

Bill injected, "It could all be a publicity stunt to save his magazine. I'm sure subscriptions have slumped, and he just can't get back on track."

We stared at each other again … for another lengthy moment … until I broke the silence with an unsettled, "Hmm."

Chapter Six

A cannonball splash caught the attention of not just Bill, Gill, and me, but most of the outdoor partiers. It was a nice distraction to move onto something else as we turned to spot two additional nudists join the pool time fun by jumping in. While several cheered, others dashed to the pool for a view.

Puffing on my cigarette I looked around the patio to see who arrived, unaware many guests were now flocked around the tiki hut for drinks. A line had formed for Brent to serve up. The crowd was thick. Views of the seating area by the manor's entrance were blocked by mingling people across the pool deck.

I looked at our drinks and asked Bill and Gill if Pinot Grigio was good for them. All in, I beckoned Brent when he had a moment, to hand me a fresh bottle. No sooner said than done, an opened cold bottle was quickly placed before us.

The three of us had maybe two sips left. "Drink up," I insisted.

We tapped our glasses, sipped twice, and I poured the entire bottle equally into our three tall wine glasses. *Cheers!* we happily yelled. And with another round of clinks, we collectively sipped.

Brent was getting slammed, and I briefly watched his charming personality never miss a happy beat with every demanding and impatient guest. One of Marc's staff delivered four large packages of new acrylic drink ware to the bar.

"Excuse me," I said, catching the young man dressed in black slacks, and white dress shirt with a nice black bow tie. "Please hand me a tallboy."

It didn't register.

"One of the tall cups you just brought in," I clarified, using my fingers to demonstrate the height.

He placed one gently before me on the bar with a smile, then returned to stacking for Brent. I reached into the left pocket of my shorts for a money clip – flashing it to Bill and Gill as a hint.

"This is one hardworking crew," I declared, removing a $100 bill to stuff deep into the tall plastic cup.

"For the excellent service," I smiled to the two men behind the bar, placing the new tip jar on the inner edge of the bar Brent's way … yet slightly to the right towards Bill and Gill.

Bill smiled with a wink. "Ditto to that," he said and added a Benjamin to the glass.

As I returned the wink, Gill made a point that tipping at residential parties wasn't necessary. I kissed the air at him to show I didn't care. And with that, I felt a tap on my right shoulder to discover Marc standing behind us wearing a black apron with white lettering that read:

FREE HUGS
JUST KIDDING
DON'T TOUCH ME

Our host appeared fully pepped-up and ready to grill with his newly added pinafore.

"Always good to see you, Bill and Gill," Marc smiled and leaned in for cheek kisses with each.

"It's amazing … but you both look younger every time I see you."

Gill rubbed the back of his fingers beneath his chin and said, "Thank you. It's the Joan Rivers nip and tuck."

"Without the fillers," Bill added.

"Well done," Marc smiled, then placed his hand on my right forearm. "I'm going to borrow this gentleman for a moment."

He then turned into my ear and spoke in a loud whisper, "Walk with me," and ventured away to the side of the patio next to the food tent that was sprinkled with a handful of guests inside.

I turned to Bill and Gill and asked them to hold my seat. Bill teasingly mocked smoking a cigarette shaking his head no. Gill also had some fun as he said under his breath, "You are in so much trouble for smoking in nonsmoking."

Laughing, I walked away to catch up to Marc.

"How's Stephan and Edward?" I asked.

Marc sighed like a man with other things to do. "I've settled them in a guest suite on the second floor across from the elevator. It's been a rough couple of days for them. And honestly, they should have stayed home. But Stephan won't go back to his house or return to the hotel ... so they're here."

He quickly shifted gears, "Isn't Eddie's Electrics a client of WC&A?"

I looked at him. "Yes. Have been for years. Why do you ask?"

Marc shrugged. "I thought it was interesting one of your client's vehicles was part of Mr. Denino's situation."

"That *is* interesting," I confirmed, unclear where he was going with this.

"I'm about to start up the BBQ, so Win, will you be a dear and go up to check on him in a little while? I'd like to keep an eye on the hysterical Poof."

"Of course," I smiled with assurance. "Let me finish my fag, and I'll go up."

"Finish your fag slowly, my dear. Always take your time with your fags," he smirked.

I laughed.

He turned to face *Smoking*. "Speaking of little faggots, any idea who the nonsmokers are looking at their phones?"

"No idea," I replied.

"I wonder how they got in," he said leading us over to the parties in question. "Oh, that's right," he fake-laughed, "S&S just arrived from the airport five minutes ago. God only knows how many stowaways are on board, by now."

I laughed.

"Hello," Marc greeted the gathering of hot dudes in their late twenties wearing fashionable swimsuits and beachy tank tops. Only two broke their gaze away from their phones for a quick glance at him.

"You all know this is the smoking section, correct?"

One held out a vape. "Yeah, okay." And went back to his phone.

Marc looked at me with a *I guess I've been told* smirk. I grinned in return and raised my eyebrows. He cleared his throat with a declarative *Uh-Hem* to get their attention yet again.

"Darlings, this is the smoking section ... and is reserved for guests who prefer something rolled in paper or from a pipe. And whatever that preference is, it burns. Hence, smoking."

All the party crashers forcibly looked at this irritating old man bothering them.

"This isn't a soda shop in a dime store where you pretend-smoke with electric candy cigarettes," Marc added before taking a beat to ask, "Do I know any of you? And how did you get in?"

A guy seated next to the dude with the vape looked Marc up and down and flippantly said pointing to the side of the deck, "WaveRunners. And exactly who is this funny looking man in a smock wanting to know?"

His entourage found the rebuttal humorous with a couple snickers applauding his remark.

Marc and I amusingly smiled at one another on how this was fun, and about to become more so.

"Wait," I broke in, "you cruise up and down the Intercoastal and crash parties?"

"Yeah? And?" One of the dudes answered.

Marc and I returned to our curiously amused smirks with one another.

"Have I shown you my new audio video app for the house?" Marc asked me.

I hadn't and shook my head no.

"Oh darling, this is fantastic," he shared and took his phone out of his back pocket, leaned over to show me an app icon to view. He tapped the phone a few times. The music stopped and the AV app launched. Marc waved his hands and began to broadcast his voice throughout the mansion's speaker system while his face was plastered across the colossal TV wall inside.

"Hello and welcome everyone! Thank you for joining my little shitshow." He grabbed the partiers attention, who erupted with cheers and applause.

"I am about to set fire to some fresh meat at the BBQ pit."

Yelps and catcalls rolled from the crowd.

"All the filets and burgers will be cooked medium. If you prefer to have your beef well done, tar tar, or bloody moo, please come over to make your requests.

"From what I can tell, I see everyone is firmly gripping their ... libations."

More cheers and applause.

"Wonderful! And OH! ..." Marc spun around to the rat pack in *Smoking* and waived his hand across the lot of them. He tapped the reverse camera on the phone, projecting the uninvited gang upon the mega TV inside and announced, "I'm over by *Smoking*

101

and if any of these people belong to someone here, please claim them immediately or security will escort them to Lost & Found out by the dumpster."

He tapped his phone again and returned his face to the TV.

"So, enjoy and be Mary!" he declared to accelerating rounds of laughter and applause.

With a few more taps on his phone, Whitney Houston's *I Wanna Dance with Somebody* video filled the TV while blasting her tune around the estate.

Marc patted my shoulder and said, "Thank you and I'm off."

He turned to the group of stunned nonsmokers in *Smoking* as S&S dashed to their boss's side. "Goodbye," he asserted with a pleasant smile.

Marc instructed to S&S Steve, "Front door foyer. Please check invites – if there are any latecomers left. He turned to S&S Steven, pointed to the dudes in *Smoking*, and said, "Them. Out the way they came in."

And with his squiggly walk, Marc made his way to the grilling station, greeting guests in his path.

Knowing *Smoking* was about to clear out in thirty seconds, I quickly darted back to Bill and Gill. "Load up, we're moving to the best seats in the house."

"Goodie," Gill gleefully cheered.

I picked up my wine, smokes and lighter, and arrived back at *Smoking* just in time to hear the six intruders whine to S&S Steven how uncool it was they were forced to leave a party they had no business attending. Caring not, I plopped in my usual seat and took one last long drag off my cigarette before putting it out as Bill and Gill walked up and sat to my left.

Bill was highly amused. "Lost and Found ... that is *hilarious*!"

And like a high tide making its way back in, Keith and Rafael washed up to sit on my right.

"Hello Bill and hello Gill," Rafael politely said with no rounds of hugs.

Bill's lighthearted amusement quickly evaporated to a smile of tolerance. "Rafael, Keith."

"Hi guys," Gill politely added with a hint of dread.

"Ladies," Keith swatted a return.

Unsure what was happening between these four, I lit another cigarette, sat comfortably back in my seat, and sipped my wine to let this *whatever-it-was* unfold naturally.

Gill caught my attention. "Win, Bill and I are going to a UAP conference next month in Laughlin, Nevada. Think about joining us this time."

"It's really quite fascinating to get the annual run down on what's really happening around the planet," Bill complimented.

"Oh, my God," Rafael blurted. "Here come the aliens ..."

Unfinished with the floor, Rafael continued with sarcastic disgust, "And just how many abductions have we experienced this year, Bill and Gill?"

"We *are* experiencers, Rafael," Bill said sternly.

"This isn't about you, Otho!" Gill fired.

"Ugh!" Rafael replied, looking away, over to the pool.

"Why do you get into such a fluff about this, Rafael?" Gill demanded. "If intergalactic visitors are not your thing, then so be it. But there really is no need to be an asshole about it."

Bill turned to Gill and proclaimed, "We're not having this conversation again, *with him*."

The two stared at each other for a moment and Gill suggested they go order their steaks rare. Bill agreed then pat my forearm with, "We'll catch up later."

"Of course," I smiled, and they left without a word to Keith or Rafael.

Rafael yelled at them, "ENJOY YOUR BARBIE QUE!"

Finding the one-liner amusing, Keith chuckled, and I took in a long drag of smoke to keep from cracking up, too.

Out of nowhere, Tom and Jerry rushed in for the available seats.

What the fuck! I thought. *These anti-smokers are now my besties?! IN SMOKING?!*

Keith groaned under his breath over their arrival – which did not go unnoticed by Jerry.

"We just heard the most hilarious joke," Jerry said as he sat. "What do you get when three or more gay men turn on someone?"

None of us had heard that one.

"A gay mafia."

Keith giggled. I chuckled. Rafael exhaled with disgust.

"Anyone have any suspects on the Barbie caper?" Tom asked.

"Half the people here could easily be suspects," Keith replied with annoyance.

I didn't mention my chat with Bill and Gill and smoked.

"So what? Who cares?" Rafael complained. "I can only handle so much bat shit crazy."

"Rafael, you are such a Peggy," Jerry spat, catching our attention.

Keith chuckled.

"I know you want me to bite, Jerry, but I'm not going to," Rafael said staring at the pool.

"What's a Peggy?" I asked.

"A Peggy is an old maid who's a bitter smart ass that believes she's the smartest bitch in the room entitled to have the final word

104

on anything and everything … and trump everyone's ass," Jerry replied.

"Like a Karen?" I followed up.

"No, a Karen is a bigot breeder who's fearful of everyone who's not white and doesn't live in the suburbs and is an overall cunt that's lost her fucking mind."

"So what? Who cares?" Rafael repeated, cracking himself up over the jab he believed he just gave Jerry.

"You kind of look like a Peggy," Keith jested to Rafael, then chucked.

"Fuck you, Keith!" Rafael barked.

I heard Tom and Jerry giggle.

"Oh look, there's Bobby Bodie the porn star," Keith announced, grabbing our attention. "He's over by the pool in the pink shorts and white flip flops."

We all stare.

"Didn't he do straight porn in the 90s then gay porn in the early 2000s?" Tom asked.

"Yes, he did!" Rafael touted like a true fan.

"Until he aged and decided to go into real estate," Keith spat.

"How many pornos did you make before you decided to go into real estate, Keith?" Jerry joked.

Keith giggled, then added, "I only did film. Never video."

"Eight or sixteen millimeters?" Tom returned.

"Thirty-two!" Keith screamed. "In CinemaScope, baby!"

Rolling with the joke, I laughed then stroked my top lip with my thumb and index finger. "Did you have a pornstache?"

"Of course!" Keith proudly giggled.

All of sudden, Rafael moaned a coo as he took in a long view of a large late-thirty-something brunette bear walking around the pool in a light blue Miami Dolphins tee shirt tucked in blue cargo shorts with a fully loaded keychain on a belt loop.

"Who and what is with *that rack* of keys?" Rafael spouted.

We all have a look.

With every step he made the keys jingled.

"Shall I rip that obnoxious thing off with a good wrangling and throw it in the Intercoastal?" Tom suggested.

Jerry replied, "That bear would tear you apart like you just touched its cub."

Tom added, "I bet he drives a Dodge Ram pickup."

Jerry added, "With one of those pair of balls hanging off the trailer hitch."

I asked, "Do gay guys actually do that?"

We all look at one another without an answer until Keith said, "Only the dykes and men with small penises do," and cracked himself up.

"Seriously," Tom injected, "how many keys does a homo really need?"

To me, this was getting silly, and I joined Keith's chuckle.

"Oh, how I loathe queers who accessorize," Rafael said with indignation.

"Says the faggot wearing Marlo & Marlowe outer eyewear," spat Jerry.

The two of them glared at one another before Keith added facetiously, "What do you bet his name is Pete or Paul or Joe?"

We all sat back watching the mystery man in thought as he casually walked over to us in *Smoking*. I smiled at the Dolphins fan catching the electric blue in his eyes.

"Hello," I greeted.

"Hey," the stranger smiled, lit up a smoke with a metal butane lighter then snapped its lid closed.

Rafael summed him up without saying a word.

"This is Tom and Jerry and Keith and Rafael," I smiled. "I'm Win."

"Hey. I'm Rob," he exhaled a drag of smoke with a shy grin.

Tom smiled and said with a lean in towards Rafael, "Hello, *Rooobb*."

Rafael purposely bridged before the getting-to-know-yas went any further by standing. "Oh! I've got so much gas from all the raw oysters; I've got to find a place to blow it out. Excuse me."

Keith shouted, "Atta girl!" then chuckled.

We watched Rafael walk over to the center of the poolside crowd.

Tom declared with dread, "God bless those people because we know how Rafie loves to drop his SBDs."

I'm cracking up – watching all the victims in Rafael's waddling wake begin to cough, choke, gag, and wave their hands across their noses. Rob burst into a roaring laugh, triggering a round of cackling chuckles from Tom and Jerry.

"Thank Christ we were spared," Jerry said.

Tom added, "The party isn't even in full steam, Jerry. Rafael has all day to orbit around this gig. Remember how he snuck up behind us that one time?"

Jerry shrieked, "Oh god! His fart damned near killed the two of us! My sense of smell was destroyed for at least a week."

Tom laughed, "That is one mean queen!"

"MEAN!" Keith screamed with laughter.

"Is he seeing anyone?" Rob curiously asked, drawing our immediate attention – silencing our group.

"Actually, no," Keith quickly pounced. "And it's funny you ask because just as you were walking by the pool, Rafael moaned a sound of approval when he caught sight of you."

"He asked if we knew you," Tom tagged.

"He did," Jerry confirmed with a nodding smile.

Rob smirked with intrigue. "Why do I feel as though I've seen him before? Like in the movies or something?"

The rest of us looked at the rest of us.

Out of nowhere, Keith announced, "I believe I have to shit." He quickly stood and dashed away.

"That is the second shit he's had to take in the last hour," I randomly said aloud.

"Son of a biscuit!" Tom spouted, focused on something in the crowd. "That skinny little twit over there is eating a red velvet cupcake!" He stood with aggravation, "I am going to get my claim on one of those darlings before they're gone!"

"Get me one!" Jerry beckoned as Tom scurried to the house, then stood to announce his trip to the tiki bar. "You appear to be empty-handed Rob. Would you like an adult beverage?"

Rob took a quick drag and said, "Yeah, I'll go too," before extinguishing his smoke.

Alone again, I sipped my wine and smoked in peace. I looked up at the second-floor windows on the bedroom wing, realizing it was about that time to go check on Stephan.

Brent dashed up with a fresh glass of Pinot and set it on a coaster before me.

Surprised, I said with a smile, "Thank you, Brent."

As the drinks of the day went down, his smile had become more adorable. And without a word he rushed back to the bar.

The glass in my hand was half full, so I gulped it quickly and put out my cigarette butt. Looking over to the splashing pool, I tried to assemble some reasoning for this dastardly Barbie plot.

The bitch of this pickle, I realized, was I was there to have a nice relaxing day after an enormous windfall this past week. And now, there I was ... about to go into full-blown Kojak-mode with my friend of twenty years – who was a leading suspect.

*　　*　　*

Returning inside the mansion I decided to eat a couple more bites *of something* before I ventured upstairs to counsel Stephan. I caught sight of the cheese and salami platter and knew this was the perfect finger food. Rafael was farther down the kitchen island with his hands on his hips like a referee. He stood next to Tom by the desserts, who was holding two red velvet cupcakes and highly annoyed with a millennial guest – all about the rudeness of hoarding something or other. I popped a cube of cheese into my mouth, grab three chunks of summer sausage, and couldn't help but casually mosey over to see what was what.

Shaking his head, Rafael boldly scolded the young-something man, "Listen princess, you are a guest in someone's home, and there is no need for harassment over cupcake consumption!"

The kid sucked in his cheeks as though that was an intimidation of some sort.

Tom saw me. "Win! You provided the cupcakes. Help!"

I swallowed my cheese, shrugged my shoulders, and injected, "Everyone may have as many as they desire, Tom. Eat up!"

Scowling at the pouty princess, Rafael wasn't finished – pointing to the stranger in question. "Tom, I suggest you move along from *this cupcake* ... in particular. It's obvious he's missing an ingredient or two and is undoubtedly half baked."

Tom took the win by lifting his chin and snooted to the kid cupcake counter, "Hmmf!" And with a Joan Collins 180-spin, he stormed off.

109

Rafael turned to this guy and declared, "Don't hover. Be elsewhere."

The kid was appalled, yet not about to move.

Rafael then leaned into him with a hungry chicken hawk smile, "You know, the more I look at you … the more I may just have *you* for a dessert." He then growled a, "Grrrrr …"

That did it. Junior ran off like a scared puppy screaming, "Yipe! Yipe! Yipe! Yipe! Yipe!"

Rather flatly and not caring, I said to Rafael, "That was different," popped a slice of meat into my mouth and turned around to head upstairs.

I passed through the crowd and shared several smiles and a few hellos to make my way through the foyer, and to a closed door. I opened it and stepped into Marc's custom-built elevator. Unlike ordinary elevators, this one was like a tiny room. Its floor was white marble and walls were covered in white tufted leather cushions. There was space for about three anorexics or two girthy guys.

Three clear buttons in a vertical line ran the panel – the top had *** … the middle had ** … and the bottom had *. And on this panel to the right were three additional vertical buttons – the top one was green that read GO, middle was red for STOP, and on the bottom next to the * button was CANCEL.

The top *** button was Marc's suite. I stared at it for a while, seriously thinking a how a line or two of California snow would feel good about now. My index finger slowly gravitated to it. A split second after I pressed it and the green GO button, the elevator began to lift. Instinctively, I slapped the middle button ** in a panic. I closed my eyes and took a deep breath and rolled my head.

The ride stopped. I opened my eyes and saw ** was lit up and the top *** button blinking alternately with the green GO button. My breathing became a bit heavy and irregular … as I knew I was truly in the crosshairs of temptation. My eyes shifted to the CANCEL button. With a slow deep exhale, I pressed CANCEL, opened the door to exit, got out, and closed the door.

I took a sip of my wine and wondered what in the hell I was thinking.

Three steps across the carpeted hall, it sounded like a movie was playing with maximum volume from inside the guest suite. I heard a woman scream and the five musical tones from *Close Encounters of the Third Kind* rapidly repeat over and over.

I knocked on the door.

The movie played more crashing and screaming and crashing … until it stopped.

Edward opened it slowly, saw it was me, and a relieved smile quickly replaced his sorrowful look. "Win!" he softly whispered and swung the door to invite me in.

Melinda Dillon's voice screamed horrifically from within. "BARRY! BARRRY!"

Marc Monarch's guests were always provided top shelf accommodations when it came to overnight stays. This guest suite was literally designed, furnished, and decorated like a suite at The Ritz-Carlton – spacious living, a stocked bar and kitchenette, oversized bath, and a separate bedroom with mints on the pillows. Large vibrant colorful photos of landscapes Marc had personally visited and taken on his travels around the world were mounted in shiny black wood frames that hung on walls covered in a soft white wallpaper textured with gentle light grey swirling patterns. Vases of fresh flowers were neatly placed everywhere.

Stephan muted the television and rose from a club chair where he watched the movie and smiled ever so sadly as he walked over to greet me. "Winnie."

"Lady Lark, if you please … Miss Stephanie," I warmly bantered.

Completely overwhelmed Stephan sighed, "I'm sorry. I'm all verklempt and my manners have evaporated."

"My god! Remember when we were young … and had so much fun?" I smiled.

"Gimme all your lovin!" Stephan finally smiled.

"Come here," I waved, and we hugged.

Chapter Seven

It was the fall of 2004 and I had just opened my little two-room office for me and my one associate on Las Olas Boulevard four blocks away from the office of a new local magazine called *Outrageous*. I liked the feel and read of this upscale periodical and since this trendy gay and lesbian South Florida lifestyle monthly had just come out with its first edition, I thought as two new businesses starting out of the gates at the same time, it would be nice to introduce myself.

Next door to Bill and Gill's Hints of Tints, I stepped into *Outrageous*, and felt as though I slipped back in time to 1967 mod. No one was in, so I had a good look around. The white diamond polished concrete floor in reception included a 60s deco white leather sofa and matching chairs, with a clear acrylic coffee table donned with two stacks of *Outrageous Magazine* neatly ready to pick up. A long clear acrylic reception desk was topped with an office phone, a legal tablet and single blue pen. The chair was also clear acrylic and appeared more like a groovy bar stool with a clear oval back than an actual receptionist's seat. A single framed item hung on one of the bright white walls – the first edition of *Outrageous*.

Straightaway, a handsome thin man with dishwater blonde hair, about my height of 5'9" in his early 30s, dashed into the reception area with a startled smile.

"Hello," he welcomed.

"Hi, I greeted.

I began the introductions and Stephan Denino and I found ourselves chatting on the sofa for about an hour – possibly two –

discovering we both had a great deal in common, including fantastic ambitions for our careers and senses of humor.

Stephan shared he was born in Philadelphia and raised by his grandmother Lana. Shortly after his mother Lynette died from a heroin overdose when he was eight weeks, his father Noah was killed in Vietnam.

Educated with two master's degrees, Lana Williams was a highly respected psychologist with an office downtown. Her husband Mason was a successful litigation attorney who fell in love with a man and came out as gay to Lana shortly after Lynette was born.

However, Lana believed Mason was going through a phase and thought divorce was rather presumptive. Rather, she suggested he move out of their large Tudor in the East Falls neighborhood and into a nice loft in the heart of the city until Mason could decide who he really was. They remained married and best of friends, living separate lives, while raising little Stephan, until Mason died of AIDS in 1983.

When Lynette was a newborn in 1959, Mason purchased his daughter the very first Barbie when it was released. Two of them, actually – one to play with and one to keep in the box as a collectible. He'd shower his little girl with every newly issued doll and accessory the second they were available so as to be a part of her life while she grew up with Lana.

Lynette had just turned sixteen when she became pregnant with Stephan in late 1974, just as Noah was drafted into the Vietnam War when he turned eighteen. Mother and newborn lived with Lana while he was off to fight in the unpopular war.

Postpartum immediately struck Lynette, and she began smoking marijuana to ease her depression. Soon after, she was introduced to heroin by her dealer as a faster way to medicate.

114

After Lynnette's death, Lana and Mason continued buying pairs of new Barbies upon their release – one for Stephan to play with and one to keep in the box for their collection.

Little Stephan loved playing with the Barbies, and he'd spend hours designing and sewing outfits and making jewelry for his girls. Over the decades, Lana's house became filled with hundreds of Barbies in the box and hundreds more custom-made dresses.

When Lana died in 1996 from an aneurism while Stephan was studying business at the University of Pennsylvania, he inherited a fortune. The $39 million estate included Mason's contribution, the Tudor home, a $2 million life insurance policy Lana had taken for Lynette when she became pregnant with Stephan, and the Barbie collectibles.

Stephan stayed in Philadelphia to finish his master's degree and begin his career in the world of publishing.

In the early 2000s, he met his partner Gregg Adams who was a loan originator with a countrywide mortgage company. They fell in love and immediately moved in together. And when an opening came up in the South Florida market, Stephan nudged Gregg to jump at the opportunity, and they moved to Fort Lauderdale.

"We just settled in six months ago," Stephan said in our introductory chat on the *Outrageous* sofa.

I shared with Stephan how my beloved Chris and I met in college and were coupled ever since. "He's a network news correspondent, but I can't say his name since we both agree he should stay in the closet – for his own safety – because most of his assignments are in war torn homophobic regions around the globe," is all I said before circling back to his magazine and my ad agency.

We discussed the opportunities our two companies could achieve. And before we knew it, a business relationship was rolling full steam ahead.

When his receptionist David returned from whatever errand he was on, he greeted me and asked his boss if he'd heard about the big drag fundraiser happening New Year's Eve at one of the gay clubs in Wilton Manors. "It will raise money for two community centers that provide healthy food and medications for men and women living with HIV and AIDS. The show is open to everyone who wants to do drag – not just the professional queens around town."

"We should have some fun with this," Stephan insisted. "More than writing checks."

Understanding his immediate empathy for this cause – having just learned his grandfather died of the horrible disease – I felt a push to commit and do *something*.

However, I'd never done drag and hadn't planned on doing it.

"Do you sing?" he asked.

I did.

Then Stephan pitched a comedy skit idea that sounded hilarious, could raise a lot of money for charity … all the while entertaining the troops … and get our names flowing around town.

"What if you and I parallel the infamous Lucy and Ethel 'Friendship' scene where they come out from each side of the stage to discover they both are wearing the same gown? We'll doll ourselves up like two gorgeous Connie Francis's in 50s style matching floral pattern pink taffeta ball gowns in black bouffant wigs with pin curls, long white evening gloves, and pearls … singing *Danke Schoen*. And with every verse, we take turns ripping pieces off of the other's gown and that person would sing *Danke ... Shit!*"

I laughed.

"Of course, we'll need drag queen names," he added.

"I'll never be a queen and won't use my real name," I insisted, "which is not to say I wouldn't be a lady."

"How about Lady Winnie C. Lark?" he proposed.

I thought on it a few seconds.

"Lady Lark. I can do that," I approved. "What about you?"

"I prefer short and sweet – Miss Stephanie."

"That's nice," I agreed.

"Let's do this," Stephan asserted to close the deal. "We're the new boys in town. Let's show everyone just how funny these two bitches can be!"

And I was sold.

After we buckled in hysterics planning the design of the breakaway gowns with Velcro seams and some of the choreography, I walked out of our first visit knowing Stephan and I were not only fast friends, but two powerhouses that were going to take the local community by storm.

* * *

The night of the fundraiser, the club was packed. Several people I'd seen at various business networking events were dressed to the nines in big wigs, clumsy tall stilettos, and Tammy Faye Bakker makeup. It was a hilarious sight in all directions, and everyone pushed the merriment further with rounds after rounds of shots.

Our act was seventh – which was far enough into the show the audience would be nicely buzzed and feeling quite generous – yet ninety minutes from the ball drop so we wouldn't compete with Auld Lang Syne. We came out singing and ripped our gowns apart piece by piece. For the close, Stephanie tore off the back of my gown and pulled it down to my ankles – exposing the strapless corset I was sweating in. Stepping out of the fallen gown in my heels, we closed out the number where I ripped her wig off and we sang one long *Danke Shiiiiiiiiitt*.

The crowd exploded with a long roaring applause. Stephan and I thanked everyone and thanked everyone … and thanked everyone.

Caught up with the high of performing and the synergy of giving, I yelled into the microphone, "Empty your wallets into the buckets here on stage for this wonderful cause and I'll strip out of what's left!" and waved my hands up and down the corset like a *Price Is Right* model showing off the next shiny prize.

Hundreds of bills of money showered the stage – tossed from every direction. And before I knew it, the crowd began to chant, "Take it off! Take it off!"

Stephanie walked over to me with a fantastic fake smile and covered his microphone to ask, "Do you have underwear on?"

"No!"

"Are you sure you want to do this?"

"Don't let up until we're through!" I shouted – gleaming in nothing but my Connie Francis wig, pearls, strapless white corset and pink high heels – and handed him my mic.

Quickly, I skedaddled over to the DJ on stage left to see if he had *Gimme All Your Lovin'* to play. By the time I returned center stage, the song was rocking I was a prancing around like one of ZZ Top's video models. The spectators went crazy. I picked up one of the tip buckets on the edge of the stage and began dancing through the crowd for more cash. As I made my way back to the

118

stage, Stephan had cleared our fashion disaster, and was left alone to unbutton and strip out of the corset by the last stanza. And off it went!

Standing there full Monty, I raised my hand in the air like Queen Elizabeth, did a proud pivot to the left then to the right, and slowly sauntered off stage.

"Let's hear it for Lady Lark, everyone!" is all I heard the MC yell over the PA system *over* the screaming applause, as I returned backstage to find Stephan holding open a white robe for me to step into.

"Danke Shoen!" he laugh-shouted.

"Danke shit!" I laughed, closing the robe – riding the high of whipping it up.

From that day on, we fondly – and privately – addressed one another as Steph and Winnie.

*   *   *

It was a record-breaking evening. The fundraiser brought in twenty-six thousand in cash and another seventeen grand in checks and pledges.

Steph and I immediately had requests from owners of several gay clubs to perform our Danke Schoen act – which we declined. "One and done," was my *thanks for asking* close to that.

For me, Lady Lark was a one night only gig. A successful gig albeit. R.I.P. Lady Lark!

Word of mouth our high-energy / all-out efforts also quickly spread around town. We were invited to join fundraising committees and boards with just about every nonprofit organization serving the gay and lesbian community. It was a wonderful opportunity to give back. It was also the perfect forum to bring on new clients.

From there, our companies simply took off.

*   *   *

Steph had told me he'd never disclosed his actual wealth to his partner Gregg, other than to say they never had to worry about money. "My grandmother left me a few dollars, so we'll be okay," was about all the assurance he gave him.

Over the years, Gregg had made and spent the vast fortune he generated as a loan originator. Gratified to be the provider, he lavished Steph with first class trips around the world, fabulous wardrobes from Nieman Marcus, new BMWs every two years, and a McMansion in the heart of Wilton Manors. But in 2008, when the countrywide mortgage company he worked for collapsed, so did his retirement fund, which he had fully invested in the company's stock. Their home was now underwater by six hundred thousand dollars – with an existing mortgage in his name alone for $1.8 million.

Too proud to confess all this to Steph – let alone discuss the idea of short selling the house or that he was too devastated to start over – Gregg closed the garage door after Steph left for the office one morning and ran his month-old BMW inside until he was found when Steph came home from work that night.

Angry that Gregg killed himself and angry he was now alone, and angry Gregg left him to decipher the financial debacle he was now in, Steph landed one afternoon at Twenty-8 to get completely smashed. As he sat at the bar and Lisa poured him a drink, he met a man named Marc Monarch.

120

A dozen drinks in, Steph shared with his new barfly how his mother killed herself with drugs … and now Gregg … and the only ones left in his life were his Barbies … who would never do such a thing.

Jumping in with a mental life preserver, Marc jested he didn't believe Suicide Barbie would ever be on the market, so he really had nothing to worry about in that department. "I would think S&M Barbie would come out long before Razor Blade Barbie."

It worked, and Steph laughed.

Marc shifted gears and wanted to discuss *Outrageous*.

Steph mentioned how Marc thought it was a lovely high-end monthly. But without directly calling the magazine a puff piece, he suggested a new column exposing some of the 'more contemptible' things the elite folks in our community were engaged in could add a little spice to the editorial side.

"Marc told me about a dozen scandals that were happening in the gay business world and their detestable activities should be outed," Steph once said to me.

He also said Marc mentioned, "The dirt always comes out on laundry day. And if you could create a column called … oh … say … *Outrage* … I would happily place a hundred-thousand-dollar ad buy with Monarch Global."

The seed was planted but Steph caught on – the beginning of Marc's suggestive control of editorial for ads; and the potential end of his popularity throughout the community he worked so hard to attain.

Steph said he told Marc he may be interested in revisiting the idea sometime down the road. He wasn't sure if he'd keep the magazine, or call it quits. He didn't know what page he was on. After all, he just buried the love of his life.

During a six-month pause, Steph placed *Outrageous* on hiatus. From a short sale, he bought a large, recently renovated home in Victoria Park on a channel leading to the Atlantic Ocean. He hired an extremely handsome Cuban named Edward Santiago as his personal assistant. And against the advice of his financial advisors, he paid off the mortgage on the McMansion, deciding to hold onto the property until the market rebounded – and turned it into a bed and breakfast to pay for its utilities, taxes, and insurance.

In January 2009, Stephan Denino came back stronger than ever. He returned to publishing his magazine by jumping into the reporting arena with a new column called *Outrage*. Taking Marc up on his idea without the commitment of his advertising – or his editorial input – Steph's first duty of business was to blast off February with a report that would shock the world. And it did.

The investigative story featured Maury Bridges, a prominent gay business owner of an extremely successful kitchen and bath remodeling center who ran a human trafficking scheme on the side by bringing in gay young men from Thailand to become houseboy slaves for his wealthy clientele. The atrocities were specific. Names were named. Addresses were listed.

Steph's article was picked up by national and global news wires. Local news coverage had reporters delivering live reports outside his office. The FBI jumped into action. And within ten days after the February 2009 *Outrage* column came out, nine people were arrested and charged.

Overnight *Outrageous Magazine* had become a global brand. Its online web traffic exploded to over four million individual users. And Stephan Denino was invited to give interviews on morning network shows and primetime cable news.

Every other month, the *Outrage* column detonated new seismic booms throughout the South Florida community with one disgraceful scandal after another involving prominent gays and lesbians and bisexuals. And while Marc Monarch truly loved the 'new' magazine's bite, one by one Steph's friends quickly became acquaintances, then frenemies ... and for many, outright enemies.

With all the successes *Outrageous Magazine* itself was having ... it was the failed friendships and zero invitations to anything except to exit boards ... that began to gnaw heavily on Steph's heart and soul. By Thanksgiving, he was clinically depressed. By Christmas, he was on antidepressants. And for umpteen years now, my friend Steph has been a functioning pill-popping alcoholic still cranking out the magazine everyone bitches about, yet still must read, each and every month.

Chapter Eight

"Let's sit," Edward welcomed and walked over to the sofa for a seat.

Steph took my hand and escorted me to the chair where he was parked watching *Close Encounters*.

The first thing out of my mouth was, "Are you both good on drinks?"

Sitting next to Edward, Steph reached for his cocktail on the coffee table. "Oh yes."

"It's Chez Marc where every bar in the manor is always stocked," Edward motioned to the small bar across the large room with an agreeable nod.

I turned to Steph with a serious sigh, "Tell me everything. From the beginning."

He repeated what he said upon his arrival at the party. The story was identical.

"Except for one thing," he paused and looked into my eyes, then spoke quite solemnly. "There was no ransom. It's more like this is a game of torture. A punishment of sorts."

Edward caught my attention. "Not a mention of money."

I leaned back into the extremely comfortable chair and took a long sip of wine.

Well, this just put the kibosh on Gill's suspected theory Stephan may have done it. I thought.

"How was the collection, with so many dolls, removed from your home so quickly?" I wondered aloud.

Steph took breath and said, "Well, my prized and most valuable girls I kept on display in glass hutches throughout the house to admire every day. But the majority of the collection was still in their original packaging and stored in large plastic tubs with lids in my garage. It's air conditioned, so it was climate controlled."

"How many tubs?" I asked.

Steph ran the numbers in his head as he spoke. "The garage has three bays for three cars. In two of the bays, the tubs are tightly lined up and stacked to the ceiling. Each tub is three feet in length by two feet in depth. There were six in a row. With ten rows. Six high. So, that would be about three-hundred-sixty ... four hundred ... give a take a few.

"Each tub housed roughly ten Barbies or and/or accessories. So, in the garage alone, there were nearly four-thousand pieces of the collection; with another hundred in my home. And another twenty-something tubs in the guest room."

I listened carefully and visualized the picture Steph had put together, then added, "So, if a very large box truck is backed up to your car space, and that particular garage door was opened, moving the tubs into the truck could be done swiftly enough by one or two people in less than an hour. And if they brought extra tubs for the Barbies inside the house, running around pulling them out of the cabinets could be done in a matter of minutes."

Steph sniffled and nodded with a shrug. "Yes. That could have happened."

"This is a well-planned inside job, Steph," I said, "Someone had to know the layout of your house and the garage ... and how the collection was stored ... and exactly where all the Barbies were."

Stumped, we sat in silence for a minute and looked at each other.

"Win," Edward injected, "you're in public relations. What if we reached out to the president of the Global League of Barbie

126

Collectors for a statement demanding the immediate release of all the Barbies being held against their will?"

I was beyond stunned. *What?!*

Steph stepped in. "For God sakes, Edward, we're not talking about the hijacking of a jet airliner full of passengers here!"

These two have fallen overboard from the Ship of Sanity! My mind shrieked.

And for some odd reason, since we were now completely off the charts, I thought I'd jump into the waters of crazy with one of my twisted family tales.

"Did I ever share with you the time my father became so enraged his front tooth snapped off and flew across the dinner table into a bowl of gravy?"

The two gave me a combined look of *What does that have to do with any of this?* and *Your father's tooth went where?!*

Toying with them, I smirked and said nothing until they answered.

"No!" Steph and Edward said in unison.

I furthered the tease without a response.

"Oh my God, you're killing me, Winnie! What the fuck *happened*?!" Steph insisted with his mind finally on something else.

I began with, "It's summer break 1975. I'm ten. My younger sister is six.

"We had a great time going up to Battle Creek, Michigan for a tour of the Kellogg cereal plant. Battle Creek was only a couple hours away, so it was a day trip where Mom chauffeured several neighborhood kids with us along for fun.

"And now we're home – me, my sister, and Mom – all laughing and enjoying one another at the dining room table waiting for Father to join us for supper. We're joking and giggling and chatting about how Froot Loops and Cocoa Krispies are made. The three of us were jubilantly happy.

"Enter my dad, who's in a really shitty mood from a day at work – not unlike any other day – but that day he was ready for bear.

"Mom had made roast beef with all the trimmings. The table is beautifully set. And as Father took his place and had a good look at all our cheerful faces, he scowled, 'What's everyone so god-damned happy about?'

"My little sister cooed on how much fun we had at Kellogg's that day. Of course, Father was unimpressed as he began serving up his own plate. I added how it was really a great trip.

"Mom said, 'The children and I had quite a lovely day, Jack. And we'd appreciate it if you didn't spoil it.'

"He froze and took a good long look at each of us with one of his detestable sneers.

"I said something rather smartass like, 'Yeah.'

"My sister copied me with a second, 'Yeah.'

"Well, there sat Jack at the head of the table clenching his teeth … boiling in fury. We watched the veins in this face and neck begin to pop and bulge like never before.

"Suddenly, his front tooth just snapped and soared across the table and went *Bloop!* right into the gravy bowl.

"Of course, we're all in amazed shock. My mother covered her mouth. Sis and I dropped our jaws.

"Right on cue, my father screamed, 'GOD DAMN IT TO HELL!'

"And out of the mouth of my little sister came, 'That's what you get for always being in bad moods, Dad.'

"Father stood, walked around the dining room table, picked up the gravy bowl, and marched up to the master bedroom with the drowned tooth in hand. We heard a door slam, followed by another, 'GOD DAMMIT TO HELL!'

"Mom, Sis and I sat at the table in a strange, frightened silence.

"Because it was summer and our air conditioning wasn't the conventional central AC used in homes, but rather, was a huge 3'x3' fan built into the second-floor hallway ceiling that pulled air in from all open windows throughout the house into the attic, it wasn't uncommon for neighbors to hear the shrieks and screaming from inside.

"I looked out the window to discover the Galuoppo family had been on an evening stroll and were standing on the street out front, stopped … listening to The Crazy Clarke Show.

"Mother caught sight of what I watched outside and said, 'Eat your dinner. I have a little gravy left in the pan I'll get for us. Now stop staring at the Galuppo's. They'll move along soon enough.'"

I closed the tale by flicking my front tooth with the tip of my finger and rolled my hand in slow motion like it was soaring across the coffee table into an imaginary bowl of gravy. "Bloop!"

Steph and Edward's explosion of laughter accomplished the moment of levity I sought to provide.

"Your family funnies … oh, shit …" Steph howled in hilarity.

"And I thought my dad was an angry man!" Edward chortled.

I found pleasure in serving up something they found humorous – today of all days.

Steph impulsively said to me, "I've thought about you on something, but never asked.

"Why … and everyone loves your childhood tales from the dark side … why have you, as long as we've known one another, injected one of your humorous stories just when a conversation has become serious or sad? I'm curious," he kindly posed.

No one had ever asked me that. No one had ever pointed this out. What a fantastic question!

"Self-therapy," I began with self-assurance. "I believe sharing the humor I somehow discovered within these childhood experiences of mine, has been a method of healing the scar tissue. And by deferring to me and breaking away from whatever is happening in a moment that is far too serious or unhappy, and I can somehow manage to get people to have a good laugh – even at my expense – is something I find oddly gratifying."

Cue the Bill and Gill déjà vu. Steph and Edward sat staring into my eyes with a dismayed sadness, covering their mouths with their hands, speechless.

"I understand," Steph nodded. "Thank you."

With that, my bridge to somewhere else ended quickly as Steph's Apple Watch binged and his iPhone vibrated on the coffee table. He glanced at his wrist and said in total frustration, "I can never see a damned thing on this watch Marc gave me for my birthday last month without my glasses! Fuck!"

He jumped to pick up his iPhone on the table to read what came in.

"It says NO CALLER ID," Steph declared.

His thumb swiped the phone a few times and he squinted his face to watch something with a buzzing sound. He gasped in horror. He watched more. Then gasped again, dropped the phone into his lap, and clutched his chest.

"Mother fuckers!" he wailed and burst into a sob.

Edward and I looked at one another with desperate anticipation.

Edward reached for Steph's phone, tapped it several times and watched in disbelief. My curiosity was about to explode. When whatever ended, he handed me the phone.

"A video came in on his Messages," Edward choked.

I tapped replay. A black screen opened and in red lettering read:

I SAID TELL NO ONE!
BUT YOUR MOUTH KEEPS GOING AND GOING!

The video cut to a row of naked blindfolded Barbies standing by side against a wall. A hand wearing a blue surgical glove grabbed one while the other hand – also in a blue latex glove – began to shave its head with a pair of electric hair clippers. The shaved doll was tossed aside, and another was picked up for a buzz cut. Then another. And another. As the hand reached for another Barbie, the screen went to black and read:

DEATH BY A THOUSAND HAIRCUTS
UNTIL YOU SHUT UP!

"Oh, God," I uttered, and set the phone on the coffee table.

The three of us stared at one another as Steph whimpered. We collectively gulped our glasses dry.

Speechless, I broke my gaze to watch the muted *Close Encounters* scene where an officer from the Air Force was holding up a mounted photo of a pewter flying saucer in midair. He was explaining to the locals and TV crews how UFO were not real.

My eyes went to Steph, then around the room. A wine cooler beneath the bar caught my attention and I got up and walked over.

I reached in to slightly pull out a Chardonnay, no. A Riesling, no. The last was a Pinot Gris I could live with, so I opened the screw top, poured myself a glass, and walked it over to the coffee table.

I held out both hands and said whimsically to lighten the mood just a pinch, "As your personal bar bitch, may I refill your drinks?"

The two handed me their glasses and I returned to the bar. There was still ice in the bucket, so I dropped in the cubes and poured Bacardi halfway up the tallboys. I opened the mini fridge for a Diet Coke and turned to announce, "There is only regular Coke and Sprite left. No Diet Coke."

Steph broke into another round of sobs.

"Regular is fine," Edward said.

I made their drinks, handed them off, sat down, and reached for my wine. Looking at the two, I stated calmly, "The question is, *Why?*"

We took a few sips from our drinks in silence and then I said quite seriously, "Steph, let's think about what you have done ... and to whom."

Rather taken, he dropped me a stunned look as if I had just called him out. Which I had.

"I'm not attacking you," I clarified, "but you have done something to really upset someone, who's now after you. And we have figure out who it is.

"So, let me put it to you this way: Who would do this to you ... and why?"

Steph and Edward stared at me for a bit, until Edward spoke up, "He's right, Stephan. Who would have motive to torture you like this?"

Steph sniffled, shook his head, and stared off into space. "I don't know."

He took a long gulp from his cocktail and finally said, "With all the enemies I've made over the years in my *Outrage* column, and all the people who are mad at me for reporting this dirty little secret or for that nasty scandal, or those who simply do not like me … boiling it down to who is the angriest or craziest to go to these lengths … the theft, the pictures, now the video … what you're really asking me is … of all those people … who do I feel is truly the most disturbed?"

"With the resources to pull it off?" I added.

Steph looked at me with absolute dread. "Winnie, that number is too high for me to count."

"Let's back up and begin again," I suggested. "Who all … *exactly* … had the security code to your house … besides you and the housekeeper?"

"Well, I know it," Edward confessed matter-of-factly.

"And?!" I became exasperated. "Who else?!"

They looked at each other and Steph continued, "The pest control company, my handyman, the window cleaning company, and Marc and Sandy to keep an eye on things when we travel on long trips."

"What?!" I snapped. "How did you both forget to mention five others … six with you Edward … who have access to your house? Anyone else?!"

Steph looked at Edward to answer the ongoing question. Edward shrugged and shook his head no. Steph looked back and quietly shook his head too.

"This is fucking great, Stephanie! We now have a board game of *Clue* in play and the only person you *didn't* give your home security code to was Colonel Mustard!"

"Please don't be mad at me," Steph whimpered.

"Or me," Edward softly echoed.

"I wasn't thinking … and I … I just forgot," Steph added.

"I'm not mad," I said in a deep exhale. "I'm as frustrated as you and those are really important details *you both forgot to mention*!"

All I had left in me was a long sigh. I suggested we go outside for a cigarette – Steph being my smoking partner at all of Marc's parties.

"I gave up cigarettes on my birthday," he said, pulling out a vape from his shirt pocket for a puff.

I smiled with a nod. "I can only vape in planes, trains, and automobiles. For now, I need real smoke," I said, stood, and added, "Let's think about this. Because I too would like to know the who and the why. And now we have more who's than why's."

"Thank you, Win," Edward got up and said, "You're a good friend."

Steph also stood and walked over to me for a hug. "Yes, you are. Thank you."

It was a lengthy embrace I knew he needed. I glanced at the TV to watch the movie where semi-trailers were being covered with "Piggly Wiggly" and "Coca-Cola" signage, then drove off a secret government base followed by a "Baskin-Robbins Ice Cream" truck.

When Steph finally pulled away, I asked, "How about you two come down and get something to eat?"

Edward looked at him. "We should get some lunch."

"You go ahead, I'm going to stay up here," Steph replied with resignation and sat back on the sofa.

"I'll get you a plate?" Edward suggested.

Steph nodded with a sad smile.

With that, Edward and I turned to leave, but I paused and turned back to Steph.

"Steph?" I gently said.

He looked at me. "Yeah?"

"Are you happy?"

He cocked his head like *Are you kidding?*

I looked at him with sincerity. "I'm not talking about the events of today or yesterday or Thursday. I'm talking about your life. Are you happy?"

Steph's eyes glanced to the floor with confused uncertainty, then back to me. "Like you?"

"Like the young man I met twenty years ago in an office with a single framed cover of a first edition hanging on the wall. That's who I'm asking. Is *he* happy?"

Steph pursed his lips. A fat tear rolled down the left side of his weathered face as we stared at one another for several long seconds in silence before he turned away.

Breaking the quiet moment, Steph asked, sounding altogether broken, "Do you remember the *I Hate You* cards and *Love Nōts*?"

His eyes returned to me, and I nodded.

"Since they came out … what … a decade ago … I have received over nine hundred. Nine-hundred and forty-four, to be exact."

I didn't know what to say and remained speechless.

"Each and every one was hurtful. And painful to open.

"You know, Win, all I wanted to do was write about the wrongs of people's sins. People we know. People who are trusted within our community. In the end, I'm being sued for liable. And *I'm* the bad guy … the hated one."

Sorrowfully, I gently asked him if, possibly, it was time to do something else … something he would love to do … something that would bring him joy.

"I don't know. This loss of my girls has destroyed me."

135

I stood and watched another heavy tear roll down the cheek of my friend, feeling helpless as he turned to the TV.

"If I could have my Barbies back, I would be the most grateful human being on the planet," Steph sighed in almost a whisper.

Slowly and quietly, I turned and left with Edward.

We stepped into the hall, closed the door and Edward asked, "Stairs or elevator?"

"Let's play on Marc's elevator," I half-smiled.

On the ride down, he turned to me and inquired in a way that sounded like he really didn't want to know the answer, "Do you think the SOB doing this is here … at the party?"

"God only knows," I sighed again, without an inkling.

I leaned my head back for a view of the elevator ceiling. To the right was a small black camera in the corner that caught my attention. Every room in Marc's place had one, two or three cameras expertly and discreetly tucked into the ceilings – recording 24/7. Marc was not only insecure about his home security, but he was also an avid voyeur who liked to watch anything and everything that took place inside and outside his home. And like a Vegas hotel, every square inch of space was being watched.

If the 'killer' *was* here, it would be on video, I realized, and felt the rush to talk to Marc about this. But he was in the middle of grilling and now was not the time.

The elevator stopped. Edward and I stepped out and I pulled a smoke from my case to fire up.

"We'll see you later," he half-smiled.

I forced a grin and nodded, and he walked away.

Looking up, I paused — carefully scanning every crease of the coffered ceiling to my right down the hallway in the south wing for little black cameras neatly tucked in corners. There were two. Slowly I paced my way to the foyer and discovered three more. And with each step through the crowd to outdoors, I realized there was no need to keep searching – Marc's Big Brother was everywhere.

There would be plenty of security footage to go over later with Marc, I concluded, just before I was hijacked by a delicious smoke rolling from the grills. The smell cut me off at the knees. The air was mouth-watering! An instant hunger stopped me dead in in my tracks and was redirecting me to grab a plate of steak.

I looked around. The line of guests waiting to be served in BBQ was six deep. Marc was soaking wet from ferociously working in tandem with the grill's flames and his two sous chefs. I thought I'd have a cigarette to let the line thin out a bit.

I strolled over to *Smoking* and lit up. There were two empty seats, but I didn't feel the need to join the other smokers I didn't know. Instead, I walked over to the Intercoastal edge to watch the breezes coming off the ocean and lift this flavorful smoke to share with the rest of the world.

The beautiful smells coming from the BBQ had quickly shifted my mood to the present. Partygoers were now happily mingling and dancing to Wang Chung's *Everybody Have Fun Tonight*. A dozen skinny-dippers had an active volleyball game going in the pool. Passing yachters cheered at the assembly of fun happening here. Yes, Marc's party was lively and oh so gay.

But my stomach growled. It was time to sideline Steph's Barbie horror story and get something to eat. And have some fun for a good solid minute or ... sixty!

* * *

137

With sweat dripping down his face, Marc placed a beautiful filet hot off the grill with long tongs onto my plate with a larger-than-life smile of pride. Cooking and grilling for 'his people' brought him the most joy of anything, I believed, in all the years I'd known him. This was his passion, his zest.

"Bon Appetit, darling!" he shouted with delight.

"Thank you, love!" I cheered in return, moving on with a smile to get a baked potato and salad from the food tables.

Not leaving my near-empty wine glass behind like I had in the kitchen earlier, I carefully made my way to the tiki bar for a refill with both hands occupied before heading into the dining tent. Through the crowd waiting for drinks, Brent caught sight of me and waved me over to the side of the bar. By the time I navigated around the thirsty line of guests and reached him, the friendly bartender was ready, and held out a full glass of wine with a kind smile. He gently removed the used glass from my hand and replaced it with a refresher.

"Thank you, Brent," I grinned with a wink.

Fully loaded, I made my way into the dining tent to find the long table was half-filled with guest eating and chatting away. I spotted Gary and Lucas with an open seat directly across from them and made my way there to dine.

As Gary and I smiled at one another, Lucas licked his fingertips and politely greeted, "Hi, Win!"

"Hello. Hello." I rolled a smile his way, adding, "This meal looks spectacular."

"Everything is so good!" Gary's young man wailed with delight.

As I cut into my filet and began to eat, I heard the words *Outrageous Magazine* from people sitting to my right. I'd seen them around town but didn't know. Gary, Lucas, and I couldn't help but overhear their mean boisterousness.

"Stephan offered me a blowjob if I bought a year's worth of ads! It sealed the deal."

"Me, too!" someone else shouted.

"Is there anyone's cock he didn't suck to get people to advertise in his magazine?"

My eyes immediately moved to Gary who was watching me listen. I continued to eat.

"*Outrageous* used to be a classy publication," another someone said. "I remember when, before Stephan began that *Outrage* column of his, it was truly a positive upscale lifestyle magazine. And like overnight, Stephan took a cool gay and lesbian periodical and turned it into a gay gossipy rag. It's been nothing more than *The South Florida Gay Tattling Enquirer* and is far past its expiration date."

"It's like he began to chew on and spit out the very community the magazine was for," another someone added. "And I made him eat my ass for an ad contract. Which he did."

"Stephan's a sad little man with a sad little story whom I could give one fuck about. And I don't feel sorry for his self-inflictions one bit … let alone his stupid dolly massacres."

"That fruit is *always* three breaths away from having a mental breakdown."

"Bet he's on his last one today!"

A round of laughter came next and the group of six got up and left. I continued to eat as someone quickly came over with a tray to clear their area. Gary had finished eating while Lucas still worked on cleaning his plate.

I heard *'He's such a scumbag'* and *'I really hate that Step-Han'* from the couple to my left before they stood and went back to the party.

The three of us sat in silence until Lucas broke in with, "Sounds like there aren't too many people who like this guy with the Barbies."

"How were the ribs?" I asked, moving to change the subject as I sliced another bite of filet.

"Oh!" He moaned with satisfaction. "Fantastic!"

"Marc is a master with the grill," I smiled.

Lucas wiped his mouth with a white cloth napkin and placed it next to his plate. "I'm going for dessert," he said before turning to Gary. "Would you like something?"

Gary gave him a cute, quizzed smirk. "It's a cheat day, why not? I'll have a crème brulée or a chocolate cupcake with chocolate icing ... or both."

"Win, may I bring you something?" he asked.

I help up my wine glass. "My dessert is right here, thank you."

Lucas leaned in for a sweet kiss with Gary and off he went.

I was thrilled Gary met someone who brought him bliss. His history of dating younger men hadn't always been sterling. The go-to guys were always the athletic – yet most athletes were looking for sponsors, or in Gary's case, a sugar daddy.

"Is he a good one?" I coyly asked Gary.

"He has his own money," he replied with an approved smile.

I smiled with delight. "That's a great place to start. Tell me more," I said and dove into my baked potato.

"Lucas and his family have a portfolio of rental properties. All their tenants pay online. He is the bookkeeper, so he balances the AR and AP, and remotely emails weekly reports to the family ... and gets to work out."

"Nice," I smiled.

Gary smiled. "It is."

"I'm happy you're happy," I winked.

"Are you happy?" Gary gently inquired.

"Do I look happy?" I teased.

"Exceptionally."

"I am."

"Is there a reason why you're looking *so exceptionally* ... happy?" Gary prodded.

He knew me pretty darn well. And obviously, he'd picked up on my quiet elation over the past several weeks in selling the company *and* the building.

We looked at one another as I took a sip of wine and decided to just come out with it. "I sold the WC&A building Wednesday."

"That's fantastic! Congratulations!" He beamed, then let a moment of silence seep in as I finished eating my steak.

"Is that all?" Gary finally asked.

I smiled, feeling better having eaten an actual meal.

"Is that *all you sold*?" He teasingly pressed with a raised eyebrow.

My gaze remained with a now-frozen smile. Then a strange awareness washed over me.

I realized this would be the last time I would see Gary – in person – *as a colleague*. I was now solely looking at a dear friend. A friend that is ... I was unable to be fully truthful with ... at that particular moment.

"I can tell you I sold the WC&A building. And I can also tell you I will have something *more exceptional* to say on Monday."

On Monday. Gary knew that was a corporate code for *Something Major Has Happened* but won't be publicly disclosed until such and such date. He understood exactly what I had just *not* said. As much as I tried to contain the rumor mill and keep the sale of WC&A far beneath the down-low, Gary had sensed for a while something was in play.

Unexpectedly, Gary's eyes welled up and he reached across the table, took my hand with a gentle squeeze, and nodded with a look of understanding. Instantly, he broke into a silent sob. Tears rolled down his tan handsome face. And I found myself beginning to quietly cry, too.

"Okay?" I squeezed his hand, feeling the tears flow.

He sniffled and nodded. I could see he really worked hard to process this was an unspoken professional good-bye.

"Okay," he agreed, squeezed my hand ... and let go.

We blotted our cheeks with the napkins.

"Monday," I said with a nod.

"Monday," he confirmed with a shaking nod, trying to make the cry go away.

I wiped each eye, set the napkin on the empty plate, reached for the wine, and gulped.

"I'm surprised you haven't lit a cigarette," Gary jested with a composure cough, drying his eyes as well.

I beamed a huge smile, snapped my fingers, pulled one out, fired it up and spoke in smoke, "I don't particularly give a fuck if I'm not in *Smoking*."

Gary laughed at my defiance with his handsome kind smile.

"Monday," he said nodding, as if repeating the day would either make this register or simply go away.

I cocked my head with an expression that insisted *We just pulled ourselves together! Now stop!* and said with a declaration we were putting an end to this, "Monday."

He nodded and I smoked ... until Ron Saltz and Steven Wolfe walked up with full plates in hand.

"Seats available?" Ron gleefully asked us with drying hair that looked as though he'd just gotten out of the pool.

"Yes," both Gary and I said in unison.

I took a long drag and quickly flicked the cigarette into the Intercoastal waters.

"Please Win, don't stop smoking in nonsmoking just for me," Ron joked.

"You're too funny, Ron. I put it out for Steven," I teased.

"Ha ha," Ron gaffed.

"Where's Lucas?" Steven asked Gary.

"Getting dessert," Gary smiled.

"Looks like you've gotten your desserts with him already!" Ron joked before stuffing a fork full of macaroni and cheese in his mouth.

"Yes," Gary happily said then asked, "How was your swim?"

Ron answered chewing his food, "It was all fun and games until I found myself playing volleyball in the deep end and began flopping around a fishing bobber since I couldn't touch the bottom."

I sat and smiled. It felt nice to be with a group of people who *actually* liked one another.

Before he took another bite of food, Ron leaned in and whispered, "It won't be listed until next week, but I have a commercial building on Las Olas coming on the market. If you know anyone who may be interested – two store fronts, offices upstairs, 8,000 square feet total. Ask will be sixteen point nine five."

I immediately thought of Bill and Gill but said nothing as the plates were cleared for Lucas, Gary, and me.

"What's the address?" Gary asked.

"I'll have that for you soon," Ron quickly answered before he stuffed another loaded fork of mac and cheese in his mouth. Chewing, he added, "Once the contract is signed."

I looked at Gary and he winked. I winked in return.

Not paying attention to who was coming or going, I was surprised when Sandy tapped me on my right shoulder with an orange same-day delivery envelope tucked beneath his iPad.

"Excuse me, Mr. Clarke," he said softly, leaning close to my ear. "May have I a moment?"

"Of course," I smiled and picked up my wine.

"Excuse me, gentlemen," I smiled just as Lucas returned balancing four desserts in his two hands.

I followed Sandy outside the food tent to a small area clear of guests where he handed me the opened courier envelope.

"This arrived a few minutes ago. It's addressed to Marc. And he requested I hand it you, and for you to bring it to him up in his suite. He's freshening up from the grill," Sandy instructed with a professional smile.

Glancing it over, I flipped it to read the label aloud. "It's from a Dorothy, Inc. at 100 Somewhere Over the Rainbow Boulevard in Miami Beach."

We looked at one another with intrigue.

"Is there a Somewhere Over the Rainbow Boulevard in Miami Beach?" I queried Sandy with an amused chuckle.

"Look inside," he said rather seriously.

I reached in and removed a sealed medium sized white envelope. Large letters cut out from a magazine in different fonts and colors read:

GIve to StephAn I. DeniNO!

"Oh, fuck," is all I could muster, tucking the envelope back inside the packet.

I locked eyes with Sandy and told him I would have a smoke and go up.

"Very well, Mr. Clarke. Thank you," he nodded then left and I lit up.

Looking into the food tent I saw goofy Ron rather animated about something that had Steven and Gary laughing. I gazed around the poolside and saw jubilant guests having a good time. I turned around to face the Intercoastal with a sinking feeling that wracked my gut. Something *worse* was about to happen to Steph.

And I was holding it in my hand!

Chapter Nine

The elevator stopped on *** and I stepped into a large alcove that wrapped around left to a stairwell going down. A 4'x6' framed black and white photograph of a beautiful, naked Brazilian man in his mid-twenties posing on a beach, raking his wet long black hair with one hand, staring into the camera yearning, hung on the wall before me.

On the right I noticed double doors to the Kingdom of Oz were open wide and was greeted by a grand foyer adorned with a magnificent chandelier. The mansion's white marble tile flooring came to circular end as short cream Herringbone carpeting welcomed one into the master suite. The walls were covered with more nude male photographs and paintings Marc reserved exclusively for his private sexual haven.

The living room was a spacious and tastefully decorated area, featuring plush white sofas, armchairs, and two short mahogany coffee tables covered with stacks of oversized coffee table books – all arranged to create a sophisticated and inviting atmosphere. The room was bathed in natural light, thanks to large windows offering breathtaking views of the Intercoastal and natural wooded state park across the water. Like Steph's suite, vases of freshly cut flowers in tall glass vases were nicely placed in all directions.

Adjacent to the living room was a smaller version of his floating bar downstairs with four identical bar stools. There was a tall narrow stainless steel Wolf refrigerator along a wall beside a long counter stocked with every bottle of liquor ready and waiting for someone's order. Above were glass shelves stocked with crystalware. To the right was an enormous wine rack with fifty red wines in waiting. And below all this were drawers, a dishwasher and wine coolers for the champaign and white wines.

Time for red I thought and stepped to the wine rack for a Pinot Noir – pulling one out on the third try. I set the courier envelope down, emptied my glass into the sink, placed it in the dishwasher, and pulled a red wine glass from the glass cabinet. On the first pull of a drawer, I discovered a wine opener. Ready, set, open, pour, sip. It was delicious.

My eyes rolled beyond the bar to a golf cart backed in by a balcony window and I paused in a moment of wonder: *How in the world does one get a golf cart up to the third floor? It sure as hell wouldn't fit in the elevator!* I began to ask myself why … then shook my head to move on.

Next was Marc's private study where built-in mahogany shelves covered the walls and were stuffed with books. A massive wooden desk made of the same grain were topped with three large computer monitors running screensavers – making the office appear rightfully executive.

To its right was a well-appointed dining area, complete with a dining table and comfortable seating for four. It was perfect for hosting intimate gatherings or enjoying meals prepared by his personal chef in the kitchenette-sized version of the mammoth one downstairs.

I strolled through the living area and into the master bedroom, floored in the same white marble tile as the rest of the mansion. It was a haven of tranquility, boasting a California-king-size bed with premium linens and assortment of pillows everywhere. A separate sitting area was in one corner facing a big TV on the wall.

I noticed large industrial eye hooks strategically placed around the coffered ceiling directly above the bed – each looking as if it could hold several hundred pounds.

For what? I thought and laughed.

As I approached the bathroom, I heard what sounded like someone singing in a running shower. I paused: *What if Marc was getting a full service fill up by Antonio about now?*

"I'm here, Marc," I yelled in.

"Wonderful, darling!" I heard him holler back. "Pour yourself a refresher at the bar then make yourself comfortable in the dressing room. I'm washing the charred meat out of my hair and will be right in."

And like that, he began to sing *I'm Gonna Wash That Man Right Outa My Hair*.

Impressed Marc had a beautiful singing voice I'd never heard before, I wandered into his dressing room that had to be no less than two-thousand square feet. I went over to the island where he said the toot would be. Its marble top was bare and cleanly polished and where I tossed the orange envelope.

I sipped my wine as I took a long look around the built-ins that were specifically designed for each of the dressing room's different quadrants: one with hanging casual attire; one with formalwear that included several different black tuxes, white tuxes, navy suits and blazers; one with a hundred pair of men's and women's shoes for every occasion; a seating area for two; a table with a lighted mirror and small white backed stool ready for makeup with a mounted flat screen TV above it airing some muted show that was directly across a seating area for two; there was a rack of his infamous Queen Victoria, Elizabeth Taylor, Doris Day and other vintage gowns; another rack with furry animal costumes; a wall covered with S&M gear, leather appliances, a three foot roll of clear Visqueen plastic sheeting, a large spindle of thick rope, and a portable toilet seat; a stacked washer and dryer; a cartoon section with Batman, Robin, Superman, and Wonder Woman costumes all neatly hung; and atop the quadrants on one side were all types of hats and hat boxes, and mannequin heads covered with different styles of wigs along the other. And at the very end were two side-by-side closed doors – one to his private elevator, the other to a stairwell.

I plopped my ass comfortably into one of the club seats – feeling like I was in an upscale clothier – and waited for Mitzi Gaynor to make her entrance.

Marc finally entered the dressing room in a white terry cloth robe with a white towel turban-wrapped around the top of his head. And I laughed at the sight of him.

Rather startled, he declared, "*What* is so humorous?"

"You have peach fuzz for a hair doo! It's the Gloria Swanson that's funny."

He paused and placed his hands upon his hips and touted, "Buttercup, if Ferris Bueller can wear a towel turban out of the shower and I feel like being a Ferris Bueller for a good solid minute, I'll be a Ferris Bueller."

I continued my laugh.

He ripped the towel off his head and tossed it in a wicker laundry basket, then stripped himself of the robe and tossed that onto the towel. The fat man again placed his hands on his naked hips and declared, "Gloria Swanson, I am not."

I burst into more laughter. The sight of him was hideous … but that aside, it was a humorous comeback.

"Stephan received another video," I reported. "It was texted to him with Barbies getting their heads shaved by electric hair clippers."

"Oh!" was all he said before asking how he was doing.

"I don't think very well. I've never seen him so despondent, Marc."

"Hmmm," was all I heard before he said he was due for one of my family stories, as he went around the room to dress himself.

"Okay then," I began facetiously, "sitting here in your sadomasochistic dungeon, I can share with you when my little bare bottom was spanked in the lobby of a Marriott Hotel."

Now in boxers with Spider-Man's face stamped randomly around its blue material, Marc stopped in his tracks, giggling.

"I haven't said anything," I poked.

"How old were you?" he asked, forcing himself to move on to select a pair of dress shorts.

"I was six or seven and the family was having dinner in the restaurant. My sister was two or three, and I was tormenting her in some unnerving older sibling way.

"Well, Mother had enough and quietly warned me to stop upsetting her or she would take me out to the lobby of the hotel, pull my little dress pants down, and paddle me in front of everyone."

"Were you wearing a little blazer and necktie?" He injected.

I quickly said yes. "A little clip-on tie."

Marc's smile read *I wore those too* and I continued.

"Of course, I ignored the warning because I'd never been spanked. It was an empty threat, or so I thought.

"I continued doing whatever a bad brother does to annoy his little sister.

"The next thing I knew, Mother grabbed my arm, pulled me from the table, drug me out of the restaurant and through the hotel to the center of the lobby filled with guests. She sat in one of those 70s big lobby chairs and propped me before her.

"Loud enough for everyone to hear, she declared, 'I warned you Winston: if you did not stop tormenting your sister this is what I was going to do.'

"And with that public announcement, she unbuckled my belt, pulled my little dress pants and undies down, bent me over her knee, and paddled my bare butt with three smacks.

"Smiling to the silenced crowd of onlookers as she stood me upright and pulled my pants back up to redress me, she announced *to everyone*, 'I gave him two warnings to stop acting up. And here we are.'"

Marc smirked with an odd delight.

"All I remember were grown-ups *everywhere* with absolute approval to my mother ... and disdain for me."

Marc said with a huge grin, "It only took that one time."

"Once was enough."

He paused for a brief giggle from my story while buttoning a fresh Tommy Bahama short sleeve shirt.

"And today those same people in the lobby would be calling 911 for child abuse!" he added.

"True," I agreed.

"Weren't you the little shit?" he gaffed.

"Indeed." I said with a smirk and took a sip of wine before asking where Antonio-for-hire was.

"He didn't feel up to being groped and fondled by strangers all day. I suggested he take the Rover and go shopping at the Galleria," Marc answered then moved onto the orange delivery. "Did you open the mysterious envelope inside?"

"No."

"I think we should open it."

"Really?"

152

"Of course. This was delivered to my home. This issue is now my issue. And frankly, I would like to know what this is about."

I drank and suggested, "Fair enough. Open it."

Marc nodded to the courier envelope. "Go ahead."

I stared at him. "This isn't my home and it's not addressed to me."

His piercing green eyes opened as wide as the smile on his face. He walked over to the island.

"Come here," he said softly.

I cocked my head with curiosity and rose to walk over. He pulled open one of the wide drawers in the island and told me to peek inside.

"You're looking a bit kibbly-wibbly," he said.

"I ate but could use a nap," I replied.

He picked up the packet from Somewhere Over the Rainbow and waved it like a small flag. "Before *The Big Finish*?"

I knew where this was going. I felt myself begin to breathe heavier ... hearing the cocaine calling.

Marc tossed the orange envelope on the island and reached inside the drawer. He lifted a very tiny gold spoon from the drawer filled with powder and went for a snort. He looked at me and did a double snort for good measure. Again, he scooped another fill and put it up his other nostril.

"Please, help yourself," he offered, then wiped his index finger across his upper lip just below the nostrils, picked up the delivery, pulled out the white envelope addressed to Stephan and ripped it open. I carefully watched him remove a white card with a large QR Code printed on it. There were no words, just the QR Code on one side.

My friend paused and realized he didn't have something. He set the white card on the table between the two club chairs and returned to the bathroom. I looked up at the coffered ceiling to discover tiny black cameras in the four corners of the dressing room.

I had enough, I realized. *Fuck it, Nancy!*

I reached in the open drawer and spooned a nice load up each nostril and sat back down, wiping my nose. I picked up the QR Code, pulled my phone from my shorts pocket, and took a shot with my camera. The screen wanted FACE ID to continue as Marc entered with his phone in hand. He walked over and sat, and I pointed the phone to my face. It opened and I turned off Airplane Mode, re-shot the QR Code with my camera and Safari loaded a YouTube link that began to play. I immediately hit pause before it really started.

A rush of cocaine clarity suddenly cleared all the cobwebs, and I was immediately feeling sharp and pert.

"We go for liftoff, Houston?" I asked.

"Blast off," is all Marc said before I hit play.

"WAIT!" He shouted, grabbed the QR Code card and stood.

I paused the video.

"This is in my place, and I want to see it the way I want to see it," he commanded.

Stunned, all I could do was blink rapidly.

"Put your phone away, grab your vino and follow me," is all he said before he snatched the same-day envelope off the island and darted away.

With red wine in tow, off we went. He waited for me at the doors to his suite, we exited, he closed them behind us, the keypad lock beeped, and we got into the elevator. I'd not seen Marc like this before yet knew it was best to simply follow his lead and watch him carefully.

We stopped and exited on the second floor as Marc burst into Steph and Edward's suite without a knock. They were now watching *Poltergeist*. Without a word, he stormed over to the coffee table, grabbed the TV remote, and shut the movie off.

As stunned as I was a minute ago, Steph and Edward just stared at this short man heavily breathing in and out and in and out.

"What happened?" Steph shrieked.

"This!" Marc snapped, holding up the orange envelope in one hand and the QR Code card in the other. "THIS is what happened. It's for *you*!"

We all watched Marc huff and puff.

Dropping the envelope and holding onto the QR Code card, Mark took a breath and said far too calmly, "Let's go watch this on my wall TV *downstairs*. Right now!"

And he turned and walked out. I dashed behind with Steph and Edward scrambling to catch up. Marc and I stepped into the elevator, and he held out his hand to the boys. "Take the stairs," he ordered and slammed the elevator door closed.

I looked at Marc wondering if he was okay. He turned to me with a wink and that naughty smile of his as the lift began to hum downward. "Think I scared the shit out of him?"

I burst into laughter. Marc hit the STOP button and he laughed.

"Now darling, this is a serious matter. Let it all out before we carry on."

I laughed hard. It was the first time all day I honestly lost my shit to the idiocy of it all. Marc chuckled. I dialed it down to a giggle. He finally gained his composure and took several deep breaths. And with one big inhale and exhale, I restored myself as well.

Marc patted my back. "Better?" he asked.

I wiped my face. "Than what?" I teased.

"That's right," he smiled and pressed GO.

We arrived on the first floor, and I opened the door to Steph and Edward staring at us like something terrible occurred with the elevator.

"What happened?!" Steph shrieked as I stepped out.

"Let's go find out!" Marc said rather punitively … holding the QR Code card high as he walked off.

We all followed through the foyer and across the crowded mansion to a clear seating area at the end section of the mammoth sofa closest to the TV wall. It was the perfect spot to watch *whatever this was*.

Marc turned to Steph and Edward, waved his hand like a page in a theater and said, "Your seats."

They sat.

We stood beside them as our host pulled out his phone, tapped it a few times to stop the music and broadcast his face live on the TV again.

"Hello my wonderful guests! Is everyone full of drink and *meat*?"

Indoors and outdoors, the house erupted in drunken screams of cheers, "YES!!!"

"I have a wonderful little ditty for our shitshow today," Marc announced.

He held the QR Code card up to his phone, adding, "This arrived just moments ago for my darling friend, Stephan Denino. And I thought the least I could do is share it with everyone on the wall TV here."

I looked around to see a hundred people inside step closer, with more dashing in from outside. Steph was sitting nervously, bouncing his knee, with his right hand over his mouth.

Marc scanned the QR Code with his phone and the TV blipped to a blue video screen with a > that read *PLAY ME*. He tapped the > and the video began a countdown leader.

4 Bleep. 3 Bleep. 2 Bleep.

It was shot like a motion picture and opened on a vintage Barbie in a short sleeve white dress dotted with small red, blue, yellow, and green squares, driving a classic salmon-colored convertible along the beach – posed with its hand upon the steering wheel. The doll's hair was tucked inside a pink scarf with a gold flower stitched on the side by its temple.

"Oh god, not the original 1962 Austin Healy roadster!" Steph wailed. "It's out of the box! It's never been out of the box!"

Immediately I found myself impressed by the production of the video. The computer-generated imagery was brilliant with shadows from the palm trees rolling over the car it passed by. Barbie's scarf and hair gently blew in the wind. The car's wheels spun as she happily cruised along.

Slowly, the camera tilted down the side of the driver's door and beneath the plastic roadster to its underside where a tiny bomb with blue and red wires and blinking miniature red-light was attached.

Steph shrieked as a hundred men throughout the house gasped and another hundred moaned.

The video cut to a wide angle shot of the toy traveling along the sunny beachside when both the car and Barbie exploded into smithereens.

The house screeched in horror!

Cut to a long tracking shot of the asphalt road and we passed over one of the doll's dismembered smoldering arms.

More screams and moans!

We came upon a burning plastic tire, a smoking car door, and then a charred foot still wearing a high-heeled black shoe – until we paused upon the torso of scorched Barbie. Her dress was burnt, her hair and scarf were completely singed off, and her face had melted onto the road.

Steph released a different, more painful scream. The room moaned again.

The scene faded to black and in red letters the screen screamed:

NOw i kNOw where u are NOw!

They all die NOw!

Quickly, the film leader repeated. 4 Bleep. 3 Bleep. 2 Bleep – and happy Barbie was driving along again.

Steph declared he was going to be sick. Marc jumped into action and told Edward to get him to the half bath off the kitchen.

I looked at Marc then around the mansion. A handful of guests appeared to be in shock.

Someone asked what this was all about. Another voice in the crowd asked if it was available on YouTube.

Oddly, the majority of everyone appeared rather satisfied by what they just watched. And the room was seemingly dark with grim satisfaction.

"THIS IS BEYOND TWISTED!" everyone heard Rafael shout. "The killer could be with us right now … here in this room! THIS IS REALLY FUCKED UP!"

158

Keith's loud voice screamed from somewhere "OH MY, GOD!" then burst into the same roaring hysterical laugh he blew out earlier.

Having waited all day for a collective bellow, the majority of the crowd erupted into unexpected laughter. A tide had turned. And now, an amused enjoyment over the craziness of it all was unfolding.

"Hey Marc, is this *The Big Finish*!?" Hollered from within the sea of people.

Suddenly, someone in the back of the gathering near the foyer yelled, "Fire! There's a Barbie bonfire out in the street!"

Chapter Ten

S&S Steve jumped on the bar and shouted to the room, "Everyone! May I have your attention?!"

Marc and I spontaneously looked at one another in dismay then at Security Steve.

"Please remain calm! A vehicle in the cul-de-sac has ignited and the fire department is on its way! For everyone's safety, please remain inside or go out to the pool area! So, please remain calm!"

S&S Steven dashed to Marc's side. "Follow me."

And we did. S&S Steven led us through the crowd, through the foyer, down the south wing hallway and to a door at the end on the right – the Security Room. He tapped the keypad code and we entered.

It's the only room in Marc's mansion I'd never seen before. Familiar with the Central Monitoring Station in the WC&A Building, I was impressed it was nearly identical – but on a much smaller scale. The room was 12'x12' with no windows. Across the back wall was a bank of six large monitors with real-time video feeds from the dozens of high-definition cameras Marc had strategically positioned in every room and around the property. Below was a long desk covered with specialized consoles, keyboards, joysticks and track pads. Two ergonomic office chairs on casters sat empty.

Once we stepped in, S&S Steven closed the door and reported, "It appears a flatbed truck pulled into the cul-de-sac, its contents on the flatbed were ignited, and the driver left the scene.

"Marc, our concern for you and your guests is the black smoke. We don't know how toxic it may be. And fortunately, the winds are from the east, so it is blowing west, away from the premises.

"If everyone stays indoors or outdoors by the pool, the guests should be perfectly safe."

The door code beeped, and Sandy entered alongside S&S Steve.

"What is burning on the truck?" Marc inquired, staring at a monitor.

S&S Steven took in a deep breath and said, "It appears the contents are dolls. Hundreds of Barbie dolls piled upon the flatbed. Burning. And melting."

S&S Steve walked over to one of monitors and clicked a mouse a few times. All seven cameras on the front of the house were brought up to show the flaming truck in the cul-de-sac from different angles.

Marc looked at me then back to S&S Steven. "Oh, my. This has become quite a serious situation."

"What *exactly* is this situation, sir?" S&S Steven sternly asked.

All eyes were upon Marc. And as he searched his mind on where to begin, I gulped my wine and watched the other front cameras showing defiant guests leaving in droves.

"They're leaving," I blurted out.

As Marc and his team quickly looked over to the monitors, we heard sirens.

"Okay," Marc took charge, "I have a house full of people I need to corral and calm down. Sandy, turn off the video and turn on some light jazz to assure our guests everything is okay. S&S, go out front and safely get the runaways to their parked cars on the street."

The three had their instructions and left in haste.

I glanced at the monitors again and was shocked. "Oh, my God!"

Marc spun around for a look.

"Steph is on the street trying to put the fire out with a cocktail," I declared, as we watched Edward run up from behind, wrap his arms around Steph's waist and pull his flailing body away from the smoking flames.

Marc turned to me and said in a hurry, "I'll start by getting Stephan and Edward back up to their room."

"I'll be out back in *Smoking*, smoking."

As we darted for the door, Marc grabbed my forearm and quickly added with a quirky smirk, "I must say, this shitshow is certainly the best one for your book."

*   *   *

We entered the foyer and multiple sets of sirens sounded like the calvary had arrived. Marc went left to the front door, and I continued forward to the near-empty bar where Brad cleaned his station. Down to a few sips left, I stopped over to see him for a refill.

Brad combed through his red wines and was sad to inform me he didn't have any Pinot Noir.

"I can get you a bottle from the cellar," he smiled exactly like his brother.

I truly hated to mix but realized it may be time to switch again. The thought of beer crossed my mind, but it would go down like Kool-Aid and I'd back at one of the bars every ten minutes. Returning to my go-to was always best.

"Jack Daniels on the rocks," I ordered, deciding not to have a seat. "Make it a triple."

"Tall?" He smiled.

"Super-duper tall, please," I smirked, observing his lips were a smidge fuller than Brent's.

I then noticed about two-thirds of the guests were gone.

"Did everyone leave at once?" I asked.

"Once the security guy said remain calm then disappeared, most everyone completely flipped and ran for the door," Brad reported.

With that, Bill and Gill walked in from outdoors and spotted me.

"We're heading out," Bill said.

"Before *The Big Finish* catches everything ablaze," Gill added.

The three of us smirked at one another without really having anything further to say.

"Let's have dinner soon," Gill grinned.

"Sounds perfect," I smiled and went in for goodbye hugs.

As Brad placed my cocktail on a *SHITSHOW!* napkin, Gary and Lucas followed in the wake of Bill and Gill.

"We're going for a nice long walk on the beach," Gary affirmed.

"It was a pleasure meeting you, Win," Lucas smiled. "Your family stories are very funny."

"Thank you, Lucas. It was so very nice to have met you, too," I smiled and gave him a hug.

I turned to Gary for a squeeze and spoke as we embraced, "Let's have lunch Tuesday."

It was a longer than usual hug.

"To discuss your exceptional Monday," Gary said as if we were breaking up.

164

Slowly, I pulled away fighting my darnedest to keep the waterworks at bay – to see Gary had lost that battle, again.

"Yes ... to discuss my exceptional Monday," I smiled.

Gary patted my biceps, sniffled a sad smile, and they left.

I pulled out a cigarette, placed it between my teeth, picked up my drink and walked to an abandoned *Smoking* and fired up to sit and watch black smoke billow into the sky from the other side of the tall mansion. Even with the scent of grilled BBQ still blowing around, there was now a burnt plastic stench swirling about, too.

Six younger men were still volleying a ball in the pool. The seating area by the house was filled with guests enjoying themselves. The two sous chefs were breaking down the BBQ station. Keith, Rafael, and Keymaster Rob were chatting with Brent at the tiki bar. And out of nowhere, a news helicopter flew up the Intercoastal to immediately position itself high above the mansion.

I sipped and smoked.

There was something troubling about this whole Barbie thing. It was a grand master plan that must have taken weeks to develop and set into motion. It wasn't an ordinary robbery. It wasn't even a kidnapping for ransom. Every detail was staged for this very day. This party. Marc's *SHITSHOW!*

My Perry Mason cap was humming.

How many would it take to orchestrate this plot?
One or two for the theft. Possibly three or more for producing the videos. But who came up with the idea? And how many were brought on board to make this happen flawlessly?

165

The code to Steph's house alarm –
That's easy enough for a good hacker to crack. Then again, nearly everyone had it.

The Eddie's Electrics Truck –
Where did it come from? Was it stolen? If so, from where? *Was* it stolen … or borrowed?

The Polaroids –
Both photos were staged. All part of the plot.

The hotel –
How would someone know Steph wouldn't stay at his house? And how would they know he stayed at the Hilton?

Steph's car –
How was it found in the hotel garage?

Why would Steph come to Marc's house?
Why didn't he go to the police after discovering the second photo under his wiper blade?

Steph's Apple Watch –
He said Marc gave it to him for his birthday last month. An Apple Watch has a Find My feature, like the iPhone … right? Could he be tracked this way?

The first video –
Obviously, it was sent from a burner phone.

The Same-Day Courier Envelope –

Was it actually delivered by a legitimate driver? Why was it sent to Marc's house? How did someone know Steph was here? Right now.

The second video –

Why was Marc so insistent it be watched for everyone to see … and not privately in the guest suite with Steph?

The flatbed truck of burning Barbies –

Why now? Why was it delivered at the exact time the majority of Marc's guests were safely in one area and not scattered about the grounds? Who drove the truck? Where did this driver go? One of the security cameras would have it. How did the driver know Steph was here at Marc's?

The news helicopter –

It's a Saturday. How did the media find out about and arrive on the scene ten minutes after the blazing Barbies arrived? Seems rather quick! Were they tipped off? If so, who made the call?

Marc's security team gone last week –

The timing of this is curious.

Antonio –

He told me he was going to freshen up. He said nothing about leaving for the day.

The video Production –

Who has the best studio to produce a movie clips Every production company in South Florida – including mine? There's also the Monarch Studios in Orlando, where Monarch TV produces its shows.

Marc's security cameras —
Why was I back to this?

As I began to think about the displays of cameras covering every angle of the property, I realized I was giving myself the spins and had to stop.

You're not Columbo, dumbo! My mind hollered, and for some odd reason, I found that amusing.

I put out the end of my cigarette, gulped half my buddy Jack down, and agreed. I was a dumbo.

This was not my issue. I am retired — set for life. Time to get back to the party, I unquestionably decided, and rose to my feet to go snort myself another cup of ambition.

*   *   *

925 and I was in and made my way to Marc's dressing room, and over to the drug counter where I rested the sweating cocktail glass. My fingers latched on to the magic drawer knob and I watched my hand freeze.

What are you doing? My better judgement asked.

You're booking another reservation at the Betty's DTs Spa! My bitter judgement fired back.

I thought for a moment and decided on two moves: do a couple hits; and after the ceremonial announcement Monday, fly out Wednesday to Rancho Mirage and dry out.

Again.

What are the buyers of WC&A going to do ... fire me for going to rehab? I laughed, opened the drawer, served up two scoops, and pinch-wiped my nose.

"Two more for the road!" I spurred myself on, feeling the first-round slide down my throat.

Up left, up right ... and I was good to go.

I neatly placed the spoon back in its cradle and gently closed the drawer. With another pinch-wipe, I heard the private elevator beep and hum. Curious, I stood motionless watching and waiting to see who was coming up to step into Marc's dressing room. The door opened and there stood Antonio in white-framed ROCCI sunglasses holding half a dozen paper shopping bags in each hand with a surprised smile.

"Well, hello," he greeted in his amazingly perfect hot Brazilian *everything*. Dressed in a tight pair of black Italian jeans with a loose long-sleeved white shirt buttoned from the middle of his tan six pack down, it was perfectly clear why his daily rate was ten grand. Antonio stepped in and set the bags off to the side.

"We meet again," I smiled, immediately wiped my nose, and walked over to the mirror above Marc's makeup table for a facial checkup. "Marc suggested I powder my nose, and I took him up on it."

"As you should," Antonio said as he looked me up and down, then glanced at my near-empty tallboy and spoke. "I'm late for happy hour and ready for a drink. Refill?"

"Please." I smiled, feeling extremely turned on by his manly beauty.

I picked up my glass and he led us through the suite to the bar. *Now, this Fifty Shades of Yummy I can handle!* my mind chimed as I followed, adoring his masculine strut.

Before he walked behind the bar, he paused with a turn to ask what my preference was. I gingerly made my way to a bar stool beside him for a seat.

"Jack Daniels, please," I smiled.

"My pleasure," he grinned, then leaned in charmingly close before stepping behind the bar to wash his hands in the sink.

As I watched him tap soap into his rather dirty palms, I could have sworn I smelled a whiff of some kind of petroleum.

"Shopping is such a dirty business ... touching everything in sight," he said as he lathered up, turning the foam dark and greasy in color. He rinsed and repeated. "It's simply nasty."

Why does he smell like an accelerant and why are his hands so dirty?

"Looks like you found a few things at the mall," I made conversation, though stuck on the odor.

"Yes," he smiled. "The stores in America are incredible. Very big. Lots to choose from."

Antonio dried his hands with a white bar cloth and said he would have the same as me. I sniffed and felt another run of coke flow down my throat.

"Simply top mine off," I injected, adding, "You missed excitement at the party today."

He pulled out one highball glass and flashed me another smile before he filled our two glasses with ice cubes.

"Yes. I had to park Marc's Range Rover down the way. The street is taped off. Is everyone okay?"

"Oh ... I think so," I lied with a smile, as he poured the whiskey and handed me the cocktail.

"Salut!" Antonio raised his glass.

"Cheers!" I smiled in return, wondering why he hadn't asked what happened – as anyone in their right mind filled with

170

curiosity would – with fire trucks putting out a fire in front of a house where they were staying.

We tinked and sipped.

"May I ask you another personal question?" I prodded with a smile.

"Please," he grinned.

"What did your parents do? For work."

"My mother taught ballroom dance and my father was a repo man," he said, never taking his eyes off mine.

I faked another smile keeping our stare going. "I took tap and ballroom dance lessons when I was a boy."

"So, you are a dancer," he confirmed.

"If I'm at a wedding or gala ... and I need to," I half-chuckled then asked, "What did your father repossess?"

"He returned vehicles to the bank when a customer stopped making payments."

I nodded, showing interest in what he was saying.

Antonio continued. "I used to work with him when I was a teenager. We'd drive out to a car that was to be repossessed, and I'd carefully break in and steal it back for the bank. And Papa would follow me in case something happened. Being a repo man could be very dangerous. People in Spain will kill to keep their cars," he freely shared.

"Same in America," I grinned and said, "I appreciate the drink, Antonio, thank you. I'm going to return to the party now."

"Of course," he smiled.

"I'll see you later?"

"That will be nice," he winked with *that smile*.

I bid adieu and ever so casually walked to the foyer, exited, and closed Marc's suite's door.

I didn't know if it was the blow or the sniff of accelerant ... but *Colombo* had to speak with Steph. *Right then!*

*　　*　　*

The elevator stopped and I swiftly marched three steps to Steph and Edward's suite and knocked on the door. There was no movie playing too loud and no one answered. I opened the door. No one was there.

I was pumped with questions. I went for the stairs to make my way to the ground floor quickly, thinking the two were possibly still out front. I took two steps to the front door, stopped in my tracks, and slowly turned to not appear conspicuous to Brad or any guests. My eyes were drawn to the keypad on the Security Room door – the other way, down the hall, at the end.

Without haste, I casually moseyed through the mansion wing to the unmarked door on the right at the end. Not caring about the cameras but more about where Marc's staff was, I looked behind me. All clear. 925 and I was in.

Standing before the wall monitors, I was taken by just how many cameras Marc had installed around the property. Each one had four rows of different camera angles rolling. And every row had six 4"x4" video recordings going.

Beginning on the left I quickly scanned the top two rows with rooftop views around the perimeter of the estate. The third row included hallways on every floor. The fourth featured storage rooms, the wine cellar, and the security room where my backside stood plain as day.

Onto the second monitor, the top row was inside the four-bay garage. Six cameras stared at the black Rolls-Royce Phantom, the black Range Rover, and Marc's glamour queen – a black 1970 Cadillac DeVille Convertible with red leather.

Marc loved his cars and personalized each with pet names: 'Royce', 'Rover', 'Miss DeVille', and the black Mercedes S550 was 'J.J.' – named for Janis Joplin and her song *Mercedes Benz*.

Antonio just said, however, he had to park Rover at the end of the street. My eyes zoomed in on the camera focused on Rover.

"You … are supposed to be at the end of the street," I curiously spoke to the monitor. "And where is your sister, J.J.?"

Immediately, I pressed a few buttons on the keyboard and rolled the time dial left to watch the Mercedes pull in and a driver step out and walk backwards.

I paused and rewound by five minutes. The date time stamp rolled to earlier in the afternoon when the garage door opened for Rover and Keith's classic Bentley was parked behind it. I hit PLAY at the normal running speed to watch Antonio walk behind Rover to look outside and think about his next option. Parked next to Rover, he walked to J.J., opened the back passenger door, returned to the back of Rover, popped opened the back hatch and moved the shopping bags he brought into the house moments ago, to the back seat of J.J..

"You already went shopping," I spoke to the monitor again.

"With Rover? When did that happen?

"And since Keith parked behind Rover, you needed another car…

"Now, why did both you and Marc say you took Rover shopping? When you couldn't have?"

I rolled the dial left to go back in time again. Rover remained parked. I went back in time to yesterday. The SUV hadn't moved. On to Thursday morning – the day of the kidnapping – the time stamp moved from 06:04:26 AM to 05:35:51 AM to

04:59:19 AM to 03:33:43 AM when the garage lights turned on, and someone quickly zipped to the back of the vehicle, opened and closed the back hatch, got in and pulled out. *HELLO!*

I stopped the video and nudged the dial to the right to let it run backwards slowly. Rover gently entered and stopped. Antonio stepped out rearward from the driver's seat and walked backwards to its tail end, the hatch opened … and it looked as though he laid something inside, next to the shopping bags. The hatch closed, and he walked up with a stack of something blue in his arms, then disappeared.

My fingers carefully rolled the dial back in time one minute. I looked down at the control board and pressed PLAY.

It was 03:32:07 AM and the garage lights turned on. Antonio walked in and over to the rear of Rover, pressed a button by the license plate, and the hatch lifted. He scooted the shopping bags over and placed a stack of something blue inside. I hit pause and turned the dial very slowly to the left … to where he just set the blue thing in the car and took a step backwards.

PAUSE! I looked at the keyboard, tapped a few buttons, and spread my fingers apart on the trackpad to zoom in on a folded blue workers jumpsuit with half an Eddie's Electrics logo sticking out beneath a matching blue Eddie's Electrics baseball cap.

"Fuck a duck!" I yelled with surprised disappointment.

I gulped my Jack Daniels, unable to take my eyes off the culprit.

"Oh, Marc …" I sighed.

I scanned the bank of monitors and spotted one video feed had the perfect shot of the flatbed truck out front covered in foam, with firemen walking about. I tapped a few keys and opened the view to full screen and turned the dial back to when the vehicle first arrived. It zipped backward quickly.

"Oops, too far," I said to myself, swiftly turning the dial the other way to slowly bring it back in and park.

I hit PAUSE and studied the frozen frame a moment. The flatbed pulled in from the left and its driver's door was on the other side – the side that was not clearly visible to all the security cameras. I pressed PLAY and watched someone step out of the truck and walk to the flatbed.

"Rewind. Go slower," I directed myself.

The driver was wearing, what appeared to be a white painter's jumpsuit, a white painter's cap, a white mask, white sunglasses frames with black lenses, and black surgical gloves. The malefactor was completely covered from head to toe knowing he was being recorded.

I rewound it to the moment he stepped out of the cab of the truck again and provided a semi-decent profile. PAUSE. I spread my fingers open on the trackpad to zoom in tighter on his face. There it was – a partial gold ROC on an arm of the sunglasses that wasn't tucked into the white painter's cap. He was wearing a white pair of ROCCI sunglasses that were *identical* to the ones Antonio wore moments ago when he entered Marc's dressing room.

"BINGO!" I cried out and took a drink.

Resetting the security monitors back to their original recording modes was easy. I placed a cigarette between my lips, grabbed my cocktail and left.

I closed the door and looked at the garage door to my right. I stood with a spell of trepidation then reached over to open it.

The room lit up 100% automatically – and Marc's expansive luxury garage was the most spectacular space for cars I'd ever seen. The flooring was a polished blue and silver terrazzo. Slatwalls ran around the room in light taupe and were covered with harbor blue trimmed cabinets with stainless steel doors and drawers. Six recessed stainless doors concealed the mechanical systems and motors for the elevators. An electric vehicle charger was mounted on the far end of the garage. And there sat Rover comfortably cool in the climate-controlled setting.

Biting my unlit cigarette with my front teeth, I stared at Rover for a moment then walked over to the pristine Cadillac. Miss DeVille's top was down, and she looked invitingly comfortable, so I opened the passenger door, got in, and closed her large heavy door. I glanced across her red leather like-new dash and felt rather pleased I solved the mystery of *Who*.

This clearly explained why Antonio's rate was $10,000 a day, since his services were far more derelict that any smut games Marc could be pleasured by. A master plan like this required someone with an exquisite skillset – particular someone who could leave the country with no traces left behind.

Marc knew Stephan and Edward were at the Hilton on the beach. All Antonio had to do was drive to the hotel in the middle of last night, casually stroll into the parking garage, find the nautical blue convertible Rolls-Royce, tuck a Polaroid beneath a wiper blade, and vanish.

But *Why?*

Why would Marc do something so cruel to someone he considered a dear friend?

Why?!

And out of nowhere, I suddenly broke into a raging ugly cry that lasted a good while. After the last tear dropped and I was done, I wiped my nose, pulled out my phone, opened Contacts and tapped Betty's DTs Spa.

An Alice answered. I introduced myself as a former patient and needed a return visit. She transferred me to an admitting nurse who asked about my condition and several insurance questions. Within minutes, a check-in for Wednesday afternoon was scheduled.

I hung up and texted my assistant Carolyne: *Traveling to Thermal, California, outside Palm Springs. Please reserve a private jet from FXE to TRM late Wednesday morning. One way. Solo – no ride sharing. No return date yet. Thank you.*

With another heavy sigh, I spontaneously realized I was angry. No, I was pissed off.

Spiraling on this, I thought I'd been in the garage long enough, and it was time to move on. I got out of Miss DeVille, closed her door, put the phone back in my pocket, slowly walked into the house, down the wing, through the foyer, and out the front door.

The sun was beginning to set and had cast beautiful pink and purple and orange hues across the clouds above. I lit my smoke and made my way down the sidewalk to the street.

The fire was out. The smoke was gone. Four firetrucks with a dozen firefighters had finished spraying foam over the burnt flatbed truck. The Metro Miami News Live helicopter was hovering directly overhead to the south, a Sheriff's helicopter hovered above to the north, and another local news helicopter hovered to the east. Neighbors were taking pictures and videos with their phones. Tom and Jerry stood across the cul-de-sac watching. S&S were positioned at each corner of the property standing guard. Marc was talking with a police officer, giving him a report of some sort.

And there was Steph – standing in the driveway, lighted by a camera as he gave an interview to a Metro Miami News reporter. Edward was meandering about looking at his phone.

Carefully, I took several steps closer to listen to what Steph was saying – yet far enough away to not get in the camera shot.

Steph clutched his chest and began wailing, "My babies! My babies are all dead!"

I wanted to walk over, step in, and announce something like, "I have a solid idea who did it," but didn't.

It was the moment I heard Steph begin to rage about the genocide of his Barbies, I decided I didn't need to hear any more theatrics and strolled away.

Marc finished with the police and walked over to me with a look of exasperation.

"Heavens to Betsy! The police want to look at my home surveillance video. I explained I was having a party to come back another time.

"And the neighbors are all in a tizz. It will cost me a small fortune to resurface the street and bring everything back to the way it was yesterday to make them all forget what happened here today."

"Why should *you* have to pay for resurfacing the street?" I asked with an air of suspicion.

"Because darling, after all, this is *my* shitshow," he declared in all seriousness with his eyebrows raised. "From beginning to middle to end scene. My house … *MY* shitshow!"

With that, he waddled into the house.

I was aghast. The usual verbs in public relation statements like shocked and saddened rolled through my mind. But for the first time in my life, I was paralyzed with dismay. The discovery my friend had done something atrocious had me shaken. And so, I turned to smoke and found myself watching the most handsome fireman remove his hat and stand by a firetruck to drink a bottle of water.

178

And out of nowhere, a strange comforting calm washed over me. I was literally frozen in time – magnetized to this man.

*   *   *

Suddenly, Edward screamed. A few steps away, he ran to me to say Steph's neighbor Mr. Swartz texted him a photo of a blue box truck that was backed into Steph's driveway. Again! I looked at his phone and observed it was a plain blue truck – there were no Eddie's Electrics logos on it.

This was a ruse exactly like the fake Piggly Wiggly truck in *Close Encounters*, I thought.

Edward dashed over to show Steph the text and my eyes returned to the fireman.

"The robbers are back at my house?!" I heard Steph scream – still on camera, catching my attention.

Edward pointed to the Rolls, which was blocked at the end of the cul-de-sac by a firetruck.

Steph began randomly shouting to the officers standing around. "Police! The robbers are back at my house! Please take me to my house!"

One officer quickly walked over to Steph and Edward. I couldn't hear what was said, but the policeman was convinced of something and off the three darted down the street. The Metro Miami News reporter and cameraman swiftly packed it up and were hot pursuit to follow the story.

My eyes reverted to the fireman.

And then, he caught my stare.

He tossed the empty bottle of water in the firetruck, wiped his soaked face with a towel and looked back at me.

My eyes are still on him. He looked at the ground then back at me.

I'm drawn to him. *What is this?* I wondered.

The next thing I knew, he meandered over to me and asked if he could have a hit off my cigarette. I pulled it from my lips and gave it to him. He took a long drag and handed it back. I gazed into his deep blue eyes as he looked into mine.

"Didn't your mother ever tell you it's impolite to stare?" he teased with the most handsome smile.

"She told me to always appreciate beauty and never take your eyes off it," I replied, putting the cigarette between my lips for another drag.

I pulled it out and instinctively handed it to him. But he paused and cocked his head as if he just walked into something neither of us were sure of.

He took a drag and looked deeply into my eyes.

"I'm Kris. With a 'k'."

"Hi Kris with a 'k'. I'm Winston. Call me Win."

"I like Winston."

"Call me what you like."

"Okay."

"Okay."

"Is this your house?" He inquired.

"No."

We stared at one another and felt some kind of magical energy swirling about. Kris took a step back then took a step forward and another puff from the cigarette before handing it back. I smiled and we stared at one another for what seemed like eternity.

"I'm at Station 13."

"Station 13 is new. Opened about a year ago?" I confirmed.

A delicious handsome smile came over him. "It did."

I smiled and asked, "May I stop in for a tour?"

"Any time. But I'm on shift for the next three days. Off Wednesday," he smiled.

"I have business in California for a couple weeks – leaving Wednesday. Raincheck when I return?"

"Sure."

"May I text you, so you have my contact?" I asked.

"Sure."

I pulled out my phone and typed as he gave me his number.

Hi. It's Winston. I texted and verbally confirmed, "Cool."

"Cool," he smiled and nearly tripped turning around in his heavy firefighter boots. He stopped and turned back for a view of me *with that beautifully handsome delicious smile* for just a second longer before rejoining his crew.

I took a long last puff and tossed the cigarette butt into a river of foam oozing its way to a street drain and walked up to the front door and paused. Slowly I turned for one more look.

Kris gave me a small wave with a big smile from across the street. I returned the small wave / big smile before going into a place I no longer wanted to be.

Chapter Eleven

I walked into Marc's manor and sat at Brad's bar. It was empty by now and he was wiping everything down.

"You look happy," Brad smiled.

"Ever have one of those epiphanies where the clock stops?" I grinned.

He looked down at the bar then back into my eyes.

"I think I've had one, maybe two of those," he replied with confidence.

My eyes glanced outside. The pool was down to three people soaking in the shallow end, chatting, as the darkened dusk skies covered them. Four others were in the jacuzzi. A couple were kissing next to one of the deck lights by the Intercoastal. The table fire pits were flickering beautifully.

I looked around the vast emptiness inside. Without a hundred bodies, it felt cold. And lonely.

One of Marc's enormous four feet by four feet framed paintings illuminated on a wall caught my attention. It was a portrait of him painted in reverse: the back of his head and backside in a green blazer and yellow dress shirt that faced a wall of wooden shelves filled with books.

How ironic! I thought, returning to the reality I was infuriated he had turned his back on Steph.

"Have you seen Mr. Monarch?" I asked Brad.

"He came in and went to the elevator," he replied.

I gazed at my empty cocktail glass and set it down.

"May I get you another?"

I fake smiled.

"I'm good, thank you," I whispered and pulled out a $100 for him. "I gave one to your brother. Excellent work today."

The young man thanked me with surprise, and I stood and went to the elevator.

*　　*　　*

The double doors to the master's suite were closed. I pressed 925 and one popped open. I knocked and called for Marc.

"Come in!" I barely heard him cheer with enthusiasm from his dressing room.

I made my way there. The local news was on, muted. Antonio was comfortably seated in a club chair with his legs crossed. The drawer was open, and Marc held the tiny little spoon filled with powder. A cocktail filled to the brim on a *SHITSHOW!* napkin was on the island marble top.

"Care for a pep?" he asked.

"No, thank you," I said calmly and sat next to Antonio.

"I've always preferred threesomes in here," Marc spouted with glee.

"Thank you," I smiled with genuine sincerity.

"For what, darling?" Marc coyly asked.

"Everything. From the moment we met at Twenty-8 until right here and now. Thank you."

Marc's face lit up rather pleased as he said, "And thank you, darling. For everything as well. Particularly that moment we met at Twenty-8 until right here and now."

We stared at one another in a bond of absolute brotherly love.

"My God! You're dry!" Marc yelped. "Antonio my sweet, would you please pour dear Win a drink?"

"Of course," he happily replied and stood, ready to serve.

"You know what I'm having," I smiled.

Antonio winked and hastily departed. The second he was out of the room, I stared at Marc soberly beneath my eyebrows.

In a long deep tone, I scorned a Christina Crawford the way she did to Joan. "*Whyyy?*"

Marc suddenly felt the light jovial air in the room become thick and not so jolly. His green eyes squinted back at me, then to the floor. He wasn't expecting that. Yet, he knew exactly what that question meant.

"Why what?" he deferred.

I pointed to the TV recycling Steph's hysterical interview on the news.

Monarch slowly walked around the dressing room to provide himself time to formulate a response. He stopped to glare at me as though he was about to detonate. Instead, Marc unexpectedly began to undress until every article of clothing fell upon the floor and he was completely naked. He sauntered over to stand before me sideways – boldly displaying the body side scar front and center. It was a gruesome incision that began on his neck, ran sharply down his arm and torso, along the hip, then down his thigh to just above the knee.

"I've never showed you this, like this. And in all these years, you have never asked to see its entirety. So here it is."

Once he was satisfied I had a long enough look, he announced rather starkly, "I'm going to tell you something. And then I'm going to answer your question."

Marc walked over to pull a pink silk robe off a hanger across the dressing room to slide on. He slowly returned to me cautiously. It was obvious he was carefully wording his next syllable as my eyes took in the pink feathered boas that lined the collar and bottom of the robe.

He went over to the island for a couple more scoops. As he snorted and swallowed, I got up and stepped over to lean into his face.

"Why?"

Turning and storming around in circles he yelled, "Because I almost died! *Almost died!*

"That plane crash was not my choice. I did not choose THAT!

"But I chose to live. I chose to be grateful for waking up … and being alive!

"I could have had plastic surgery to make all this ugliness go away … but I kept it … to look at every morning … TO REMIND ME OF GRATITUDE!"

He broke for a sip of his drink, which dribbled across the island to his mouth.

"Stephan has had a lack of gratitude. For everything meaningful. Especially LIFE!

"And goddammit, that man had no right to threaten me with suicide – in my own house!"

He stomped to the other side of the dressing room. "SUICIDE IS NOT MY SHITSHOW!"

And then he stopped. And we stared at one another in silence.

"I HAVE NO TOLERANCE FOR THAT!" he fitfully screamed, slapping both thighs with both hands.

We shared another long stare.

Antonio walked in holding cocktails and Marc flitted his fingers to coolly shoo him away. I stared at Monarch and wished I was handed that drink.

He slowly walked back to me, and calmly continued. "About a month ago, Stephan came over for his birthday dinner. It was just he and I. Edward was on a business trip to Chicago.

186

"Stephan was fully depressed over every aspect of his life – personally and professionally.

"So, I thought I would serve up some laughs to spark a little vigor in him.

"We're standing in the kitchen after supper, and I brought out a cake in the shape of a large hard on with big balls in hopes it would lighten his spirits.

"I lit a birthday candle on the tip of the dick and asked him to make a wish and blow it out.

"He did … without catching the humor whatsoever. So, I pulled a couple small plates from the cabinet and asked what he wished for.

"Stephan said he didn't want to do this anymore.

"'Do what?' I asked.

"'Report people's bullshit. Publish. Get out of bed. Breathe. Live.' He confessed.

"I joked that no one wants to do another birthday at our age and tomorrow was another day … and he should try to move onto something else if he no longer felt the joy of publishing.

"He told me he was in the middle of three bogus lawsuits for liable. He was unhappy and blah, blah, blah.

"Then he picked up the cake knife I had set out, raised it to his neck, and pressed the sharp tip into his left carotid artery. A tiny little droplet of blood oozed onto the blade.

"We stared at each for a very long minute before I told him quite calmly, 'You are not going do an express checkout in my kitchen and be a ghost in my new house.'

"I reached over and slowly wrapped my fingers around his hand holding the knife, pulled it away from his neck, removed it from his grip, and carefully set it on the counter.

"Then I called him an ungrateful little fuck and told him I was not going to run a therapy session.

"'I'm not qualified and that's what you pay your therapist for,' I clearly stated, stunning him into a speechless wide-eye stare.

"I asked Stephan what it would take for him to come back to the living.

"His response was zilch. Nada.

"'Then as your friend, I'll have to go in another direction,' I said, and told him I was going to serve up a nice slice of fucking Happy Birthday ... we were going to enjoy this cake with a hefty slab of vanilla Häagen-Dazs ... and would never discuss this moment again.

"Stephan sat down, ate his dessert, opened a couple birthday gifts, and that was that."

Marc and I stared at each other until I finally expressed, "So, the direction you chose was to teach him a lesson on appreciation by taking away and destroying all that mattered most in the world to him – his collection."

"I showed him how to not fall out of the sky and die," Marc desperately exhaled.

I smiled unhappily at him with a nod. Then I looked to the carpet below my feet and shook my head no.

"Marc," I sighed, "My mother ... my manic-depressive bipolar mother ... threatened our entire household with threats she could or should kill herself. For decades! And to this day, she still does!

"It's a horrifying thing to hear someone say ... especially from a parent. It's even more traumatizing when you're a child and live in the constant fear it may or may not come true. *I KNOW*!

"And in all reality, there is nothing anyone can do except pray to God the unbalanced find a mental health professional to guide them out of the pits of despair and back to clarity.

"I understand what your objective was but the way you went about this with Stephan was not only extremely dangerous, it was *unconscionable!*"

"Ah!" Marc popped, ignoring me, now watching the muted live interview on the news with a chyron footer: *STOLEN BARBIES RETURNED SAFELY.* Stephan was stealing the scene with rolling tears of joy his babies were home safe and sound.

Marc declared, "There it is ladies and gentlemen, right on the 6 o'clock news … *The Big Finish!*"

It was if he hadn't heard a single word come out of my mouth.

I gazed away, trying to reel in my emotions over all this. Then I glanced back at Marc who was now carefully studying me with his brilliant green eyes like a snake before it swallowed a little bunny whole.

I spoke. "I think what you have just done to Steph is as demented as your *I Hate You* cards idea."

His eyes squinted tighter. "And that Love Nōts *idea of yours* made us both a tidy fortune, my little pretty!"

Having gone off point, my lips pressed together.

"You're looking at me as if I should apologize," he assumed. "I believe I explained The Apology Tour was over."

"I'm not the one who deserves an apology."

"You think what I did was wrong," Marc added as he lifted his chin like it were a dare.

I chortled over his brazen audacity.

"Marc, you broke laws that emotionally destroyed your friend *FOR THREE DAYS!* And for what? To snap him out of a depression that has had a stranglehold over him for years?"

"Sometimes a good shock is the best cure," he countered.

"You are not getting this!" I shouted. "How could you ethically do that to someone who trusts you?!"

He looked away. "No real crime has been committed. As far as ethics go, that's a matter of interpretation."

My jaw dropped from shock and I finally spoke then yelled. "You are a genius. You are also *certifiable*!"

I was tired of screaming. I was tired of it all. But mostly, I was distraught with the reality my friend was a monster.

Calmly, I added, "The plastic doll torture and murders – in and of itself – is beyond disturbing. And frankly, it's deplorable on so many levels."

"What are you saying to me, Mr. Clarke?" the man I thought I knew challenged.

Straight in his eye I said to him condescendingly, "Nice shitshow, Marc. You've outdone yourself. I'm going home."

He pursed his lips and flared his nostrils. And with that, I turned around and left.

"How did you piece it together, Win?" he fired off.

I raised my left arm and pointed to the small black camera in the ceiling corner as I walked away. "You have a nice video of me alone in your Security Room watching all the evidence you undoubtedly will destroy."

"It was all with the best of intentions!" Marc yelled to my backside.

Not wanting to hear another word, I burst into song with Dolly Parton's *9 to 5*, strolled past Antonio sitting on a sofa, through the foyer, down the marble stairwell, and out the front doors … sadly relieved to be done with this rich man's game.

Preview:
WHAT PAGE Are We On?
2. DEATH IN HICKSVILLE
Prologue

I was sixteen and had gotten home from working the 4pm-close shift at Balls & Beers – a bowling alley my Aunt Darceline owned in Hicksville, Indiana. Mom and Dad played Wednesday Bridge at the country club and competed fiercely with other members who also took the game intensely seriously. The lights were out in the kitchen, so I thought they had already come home and gone to bed. I poured a glass of chocolate milk before turning in myself. It was after all a school night.

As I gulped in the dark, from the shadows I watched our white Persian cat, Zsa Zsa, rest peacefully in a slumberous curl upon the top step of the lengthy elegant 60s contemporary mansion staircase – until we were both horror-struck by an exploding murder scream. The kitty darted into the second-floor bedroom wing and returned in a hasty getaway charging for its life down the stairs and running to hide.

Suddenly, my mother – a beautiful brunette in her mid-forties bulging out of a black lace bra, slimming black support-top panty hose, and glamorously draped in jewels – burst upon the landing as though she were taunting a serial killer. Positively hysterical, she stopped and spun around to ensure her traumatizer was still hot on her heels.

He was.

My father and she locked eyes upon one another. And with a furious breath of air, she spontaneously grabbed fistfuls of her early 70s quadruple-decker hairdo and shrieked, "I should just kill myself!"

My distinguished father in his late forties, stormed from behind in a clean white undershirt, green and white polka dot boxer shorts and black socks, clenching the remains of a cocktail angrily puffing a cigarette between his teeth. His enraged scowl shifted to an evil smirk as he caught sight of her standing on the very edge of the top step. It was clearly apparent he saw a fantastic plunge was merely inches behind her vulnerable toes.

Closing in, Dad pulled the smoke from his mouth and stretched out his hand with the burning cigarette towards her projecting chest. He stepped into her personal space and coolly stopped. He stepped in tight. And tighter yet, until his lips nearly caressed the lobe of her left ear. It appeared they were pulled into a moment of angry breath making.

With a livid scowl Mother slowly glanced downward – catching Dad holding his cigarette above her cleavage as if it were an ashtray. She took a breath, afraid of what he might do, then heard him snarl, "Go right ahead."

Mom carefully watched him slowly pull back to deeply gaze into her angry eyes. And with a cocky grin, he left her at the landing, venturing onward down the stairs.

Stunned, Mom huffed, *"What did you say?"*

Dad waved her off with his cocktail glass, grumbling, "You heard me."

Lost in a moment of dismay, Mother instinctively clutched her plump pretties as her rage reignited. She ground her brilliant white teeth into a detestable sneer and viciously spun around to release a declaration-of-war screech to Dad's backside.

The air was hijacked by the scream until her partner-in-offenses reached the foyer landing below. Annoyed with the

194

theatrics, Dad did an about-face and waited until her lungs had given all they could. The second she took a mouthful of air, he yanked control of the floor by releasing a long-winded fart, shook the ice in his cocktail glass to her and growled, "Go ahead! Blow your head off for all I care!"

Mom grabbed both sides of her head, shot him with another ferocious scream of desperation, then ripped her wig off and randomly threw it – accidentally striking one of the six decorative wall sconces hanging on the wall close to where she stood on the second floor. The hair bomb blasted five random loose squares of glass fixture across the staircase with a soft tinkle.

Dad cracked a laugh at the irony and gave her a round of applause by tapping his wedding ring against the cocktail glass.

"That's a good one."

"I want a divorce!" she screamed.

"I'd rather you just kill yourself," he fired back.

Aghast, she repeated again, "*What did you say*?"

Dad had had it and double-timed it up the stairs, carefully dodging random pieces of the glass, stopping just below Mom's panting nostrils – and glared upwards into her eyes.

"Think about how good that would be for us. We'd both be put out of your misery."

I could see her eyes shift to the long flight of stairs behind him and visibly had a sinful thought. I'm sure Dad crimped his eyebrows and pursed his lips – realizing Mom was having the exact fantasy he had a minute earlier.

Caught, she grinned … and slowly and deliberately made a point of glancing back down the stairwell then back into his dark brown eyes. "You're absolutely right. One of us needs to be put out of my misery."

Mother smiled confidently before sporting a one-eighty room exit, slapped a bank of light switches that shut off the entire second floor lighting, and strutted into the dark bedroom wing.

Father turned in dismay over how quickly the power shifted. He glanced at the lit broken sconce on the wall draped with a battered wig and realized she had just won that battle.

Belting out a smart chuckle he headed back down the stairs and unknowingly stepped on one small glass square. His foot skid from beneath him.

And, watching Dad's painful thump and thud, and the shattering of his cocktail glass, I was horrified by the splat his body made when it smacked the tiled foyer.

"Oh ... fuck," he moaned.

Oh fuck, was right!

Preview:
WHAT PAGE Are We On?
2. DEATH IN HICKSVILLE
Chapter One

"How are you doing today?" chirped Norene Smith, the Admissions Coordinator at Betty's as she placed a black leather box in the shape of a safe deposit box on her desk to the left.

"Absolutely fantastic, thank you." I beamed. "How are you?"

Norene smiled, "I'm retiring, and this is my last day."

"Congratulations! That's wonderful," I praised, pleased for her.

"How do you *feel*?" she asked.

"Healthy. Clear. Happy." I smiled, riding a natural high after twelve days of drying out with nothing to do but tend to but my soul.

Norene looked me in the eyes with a weathered face baring very little makeup and smiled. "Good. That's really good, Win."

I watched her open the lid and reach inside for my billfold and phone to hand to me.

"We charged your phone early this morning. And like your prior visit, I ask you to please turn it on to ensure it's working properly."

I stared at its black screen, realizing the last time I turned it on following a couple weeks of being powered down, the thing exploded with messages galore.

"How about I do this on my flight?" I suggested.

She stared at me with a look that insisted I comply.

I stared back until I succumbed and turned the thing on. As it booted up, Norene focused on the file folder on her desk and opened it to present a 75-page bill for review.

"Not all of the expenses were covered by your insurance so I would like you to go over the balance due."

"Of course," I nodded, knowing the drill … seeing my phone was awake and ready for my face to open.

She set the stack of papers before me with the top sheet showing the final tally. There was no way I was going to comb through a bill thicker than my laptop, so I reached inside my billfold and handed her my black card to process.

"No need to review," I said lightly tapping the invoice. "If that's the number, that's the number."

Norene blandly smiled and swiped the card on her computer as I picked up my phone to activate it with my freshly shaved mug. Knowing it was going to blow, I turned off the volume and vibration notification setting, and placed it back on her desk.

Ms. Smith handed me the credit card as a printer behind her hummed then kicked out a piece of paper. As she passed me a premium craftsmen pen to sign for my stay, I glanced at the iPhone to see numbers escalating rapidly on each of the Messages, Phone, Voicemail, and Mail icons. Suddenly, the screen switched to Aunt D! CALLING.

I froze. Staring in hard disbelief.

"Looks like you have a call coming in," Norene said looking at my phone as she gently placed the receipt before me.

My eyes remained on CALLING.

"How about you begin this day of clarity by answering?" she instructed.

I looked at her as the phone continued to silently ring. She gave me a look: *Answer it!*

Slowly I picked up the phone and did.

"Hello, Darceline."

"Have you checked out yet?" she said in a deep throaty Brenda Vacarro voice.

"How do you know where I am?"

A hearty laugh broke into the phone followed by a slurpy cough. "I've canceled your flight to Fort Lauderdale and my jet is waiting for you at Jacqueline Cochran Airport. A driver should be there to take you to the airport. You're needed."

"Aunt D., I have business to tend to ..."

"Yes, you do. Here! I'll personally pick you up when you land."

"But ..." is all I could say before she ended the call.

I stared at the phone in shock and Norene whimsically smiled, "Everything good?"

I looked at her and instantly felt a sense of dread. "I'm going home."

"That *is* good," she remarked patronizingly as she pointed to the line on the receipt for my signature.

Shocked and stunned, I signed the bill, and tucked the credit card into my wallet. Norene stuffed the stack of itemized charges and receipt into a cream 9x12 envelope with Betty's logo and stood, handing the packet to me.

"Let's meet at the entrance and I'll have your luggage brought up."

"Thank you," I stood and said with a sudden need for a strong drink.

Norene walked me from of her office in Administration, through a locked door she quietly buzzed, to the lobby where a black Escalade was parked outside. I strolled like a zombie through the entrance doors and reached for a cigarette to fire up.

"Mr. Clarke?" A tall man asked as he stepped around from the back of the vehicle.

"Yes."

"Mr. Clarke, I'm Gerard. Your driver to the airport today."

"Hi," I smiled and puffed. "Luggage is on its way."

"Very well," Gerard said and remained in a chauffeur stance.

As I walked off to smoke my mind raced knowing I'd been summoned by The Matriarch. The Boss. Queen Darceline – the 94-year-old woman who ran the family roost, and never called unless there was bad news. Or something she wanted.

I overthought and paced.

Had something happened?
How did she know where I was?
How did she know to call the moment I turned my phone on?
This is not good.
You've been hijacked back to Hicksville!
Why?
What does she want?
So much for peaceful calm!
How did she know where I was?

I sucked on my cigarette so strongly it became hot-boxed and my lungs were feeling the burn. But it didn't matter. Life had spontaneously shifted directions in sixty seconds and was now heading South. I felt it as intensely as the hot desert heat on that Southern California morning.

Gerard called me back to reality as he held open the door to the back seat. "Your luggage is all in," he announced with a smile.

Norene Smith stood inside the glass door waving as I felt a knot ball up in my gut and heard the driver speak again.

"Are you ready, Mr. Clarke?"

Meet Oscar Rogers
at

WhatPageAreWeOn.com

Did you enjoy the party?
Your review makes a difference.

Made in the USA
Columbia, SC
10 December 2023

27444046R00117